wishful thinking

ALSO BY ALEXANDRA BULLEN

Wish

wishful thinking

A NOVEL BY ALEXANDRA BULLEN

Point

alloy**entertainment**
Produced by Alloy Entertainment
151 West 26th Street
New York, NY 10001

ISBN 978-0-545-13908-3

Library of Congress Cataloging-in-Publication Data

Bullen, Alexandra.
Wishful thinking : a novel / by Alexandra Bullen. — 1st ed.
p. cm.
Sequel to: Wish.
Summary: Adopted as a baby, lonely eighteen-year-old Hazel Snow always
yearned to know her origins, and with the help of a magical seamstress, Hazel
wishes her way into an alternate life on Martha's Vineyard with the mother
she never knew.
ISBN 978-0-545-13907-6
[1. Identity—Fiction. 2. Mothers and daughters—Fiction.
3. Wishes—Fiction. 4. Space and time—Fiction. 5. Magic—Fiction.
6. Martha's Vineyard (Mass.)—Fiction.] I. Title.
PZ7.B91255Wjt 2011
[Fic]—dc22
                                        2010024352

12 11 10 9 8 7 6 5 4 3 2 1   12 13 14 15 16 17/0

Printed in the U.S.A.   40
First paperback edition, January 2012

In Memory of My Grandmothers:
Catherine Krokidas and Betty Bullen

*T*he morning that Hazel Snow turned eighteen began like any other morning.

Which is to say, it sucked.

For a late-December baby, this was pretty much par for the course. While the rest of the world slept off their holiday hangovers, just in time to settle on plans for New Year's Eve, Hazel was used to quietly welcoming another year on her own. For Hazel, "welcoming" typically involved trying not to give the day much thought, and working up just enough enthusiasm to hope that the coming year would be any less miserable than the one that had just passed.

This year was no different. After snoozing through her alarm three times, Hazel finally dragged herself up from the crooked futon she'd been sleeping on for the past few months and arched her long, slender arms overhead.

The futon was supposed to be temporary. That's what Roy, Hazel's sort-of stepdad, had said when he'd brought her home from the city. Roy was always calling things temporary, as if his life was full of phases and any day now, this, too, would pass.

But the futon, an old flea-market find missing half its fake-wooden slats, was still there. And so was Hazel. She'd made a deal with Roy to finish high school in San Rafael, the sleepy northern California town where he'd been renting a basement apartment, as long as she could save up to get a place of her own after graduation. With less than a semester to go, and a constant crick in her neck from the lumpy mattress, graduation couldn't come soon enough.

Hazel drew back the green-and-white checkered curtains to let in the gray morning light. An old radiator in the corner clicked and hissed as she slid into her favorite faded black jeans, still soggy at the hems from trudging through yesterday's puddles. She couldn't remember the last time she hadn't woken up to rain.

After brushing her teeth and pinning back a few of the front pieces of her shoulder-length blond hair, she glanced at her reflection. Her reddish roots were growing out and she made a mental note to swipe another box of Nice 'n Easy the next time she stocked the hair-care aisle at the pharmacy where she worked. So far, she'd spent every day of winter break there, which might have been disappointing if she'd had anywhere else to be.

And that's when she remembered.

Wasn't eighteen supposed to feel like *something*?

Hazel's gaze traveled up to the corner of the square mirror. Tucked against the glass was a washed-out Polaroid of a woman in a yellow apron, a chubby-faced baby clinging to one hip. It was the only picture Hazel had of herself with Wendy, the chef who had adopted Hazel as a newborn and died soon after, when her restaurant burned to the ground. Hazel was not even one at the time, and didn't remember anything about her adoptive mother. But she knew, somehow, that eighteen would feel different if Wendy were still around.

Downstairs, Roy was watching basketball highlights, and he turned down the volume as she shuffled past on her way to the kitchen. This, she assumed, was probably supposed to be some sort of present.

"Morning," he grunted, scratching at the edges of his scruffy, rust-colored beard. He'd been trying to grow it out since the beginning of fall and kept asking what she thought. It was almost—but not actually—funny, how interested he was in her opinion these days. All of the times she'd lived with him before, she could have walked around the house with a tambourine taped to each hand and a neon sign flashing across her forehead, and he probably wouldn't have given more than a sideways glance from his permanent slouch on the sofa.

"Morning," Hazel muttered back, wedging a bowl out of the wire dish rack and using one moth-bitten sleeve to wipe it dry. She poured herself a bowl of Cheerios and ate, as she always did, standing at the kitchen sink, staring out the window.

"I can drive you to work, if you want," Roy offered from the couch, his spoon scraping at the last bit of milk, puddled in one corner of the bowl.

"No, thanks," Hazel replied automatically, turning on the tap and filling a Dixie cup with water. She swallowed it down in one gulp, praying the whole ride-discussion was over. Roy claimed he'd been sober for a year before he asked Hazel to come back, and she hadn't so much as seen him in the same room with a bottle of cough syrup since. But that didn't mean she was ready to drive with him again.

"All righty."

Roy said "all righty" when he didn't know what else to say. Which meant he said it a lot. She heard the squeak of the couch springs as Roy got up, and felt him puttering around the kitchen behind her.

"Here," Roy said suddenly. She turned to find him laying a brown envelope on the kitchen table. He shuffled to the door, pulling his Giants hat down over his head. Tufts of dark, curly hair pushed out over the tops of his ears, like leafy ferns stretching toward the sun.

"Happy birthday, Hazel," he said to the doorknob as he pulled it toward him. A burst of wet, cool air settled on the kitchen like a mood, and before Hazel could say anything—if she'd even had anything to say—Roy was gone.

Hazel stared at the envelope, as if expecting it to talk, or walk away. She couldn't think of the last time Roy had even remembered her birthday, let alone marked it with any kind of sentimental gesture.

Hazel dropped her bowl in the sink and sat down at the table, turning the envelope over in her hands. It was bigger than a regular envelope, and didn't have any markings on it. No Hallmark seal or cheesy cartoon like the ones they sold at the pharmacy. She ran her finger under the fold, her breath catching in the back of her throat. A part of her wanted to just throw the envelope away, maybe even toss it on top of the trash so Roy could see it there, unopened. He'd left her, not once, not twice, but *three* times, with perfect strangers. Eight different schools, from Santa Cruz to Santa Rosa. Seven good-byes to friends she didn't even bother making anymore.

What card could possibly make up for all that?

But the not-knowing was too much. She flicked her finger up at one edge and tore back the thin paper, ripping the envelope in half and pulling out what was inside.

Not a card but a white piece of paper, folded twice.

Of course Roy hadn't bought her a card. Hazel rolled her eyes at her own idiotic imagination. A square yellow sticky note fluttered to the table, and Hazel leaned over to read it. Her stomach clenched into a knot as she recognized what could only be Wendy's curlicue script.

Give to Hazel on her 18th birthday.

A distant ringing filled Hazel's ears as she ran her hand over the smooth paper, carefully unfolding it.

It was an official-looking document, with small, boxy type and underscored lines. BIRTH CERTIFICATE was scrolled in fancy script at the top. The date: eighteen years ago, today. The hospital: St. Mary's, San Francisco. The rest of the words blurred like a foreign language, her eyes scanning to the bottom of the page.

Two words, the question she'd lived with every day and every night, long after she'd stopped asking it out loud:

Birth. Mother.

And the next two words, the answer:

ROSANNA SCOTT.

1

Three Months Later

"We're closed."

Hazel stood on the inside of a heavy glass door, squinting in the musty dark of what appeared to be an abandoned dry cleaner's shop. She had a funny feeling about this seamstress situation. First of all, a seamstress? She'd heard of tailors and designers, but a *seamstress*? The word made her think of a plump old lady with full skirts and a mouthful of needles. But this seamstress, the one hidden in the back of a grimy storefront, lounging on an old, ratty sofa and reading a glossy paperback, was neither old nor plump. No, she was young, though it wasn't immediately clear how young—maybe Hazel's age, maybe a youngish-looking thirty—and she looked to be in dire need of a cheeseburger.

Second, there was the issue of the business card.

It had been three months since Hazel discovered the name of her birth mother, and almost exactly as long since the Google search that changed her life. Because, according to the Internet, not only did "Rosanna Scott" still live in San Francisco, but she was an active member of an elite group of artists/philanthropists, and just happened to be hosting a fundraising event at a restaurant in the Ferry Building, on Sunday, March 26, at seven o'clock in the evening.

This, Hazel knew, was where she would meet her mother. As if the decision had already been made for her, she knew she would have to go. And just as clearly, she knew what she would wear.

It wasn't like she had a closet full of options. Hazel owned one dress, and it was a fluke that she even had it. She'd found the dress over a year before, in a thrift store attached to a fancy private school in the Haight. She had been, at the time, living with a foster family on Oak Street, an older Swiss couple that ran a bed-and-breakfast for aging-hippie artist-types. On her walk home from her own boring public school, she would pass Golden Gate Prep, and often stare in through the gates at the fashionable students, each toting a personalized laptop and climbing in and out of expensive-looking cars.

One spring day, she noticed the school's thrift store. She hadn't even gone in looking to buy anything. But the dress found her, from under a pile of broken shoes in the bargain bin. It was definitely brighter than anything else she owned (mostly because everything else she owned was black), and she wasn't even sure it would fit. But something about that dress just wouldn't let her leave it behind.

So she bought it, brought it home, hung it up at the back of her closet, and promptly forgot about its very existence. When Roy brought her back to San Rafael, she'd almost left it hanging there, but again something told her to pack the dress. She couldn't imagine ever having an excuse to wear such a sleek, fancy, and all-around non-Hazel article of clothing, but it had started to mean something to her. And so she tossed it at the top of her bag, lugged it to Roy's, and found a new closet in which to tuck it deep inside.

When she decided she would be going to Rosanna's event, she dug the dress out and hung it outside the closet door, where she could see it. Because now she knew it was more than a dress. It was a symbol.

Pretty much everything in Hazel's life had stayed the same since the day she learned her birth mother's name: She went to school, she went to work, she avoided Roy, she took the bus. But inside, something major had changed. She was different. And the dress was the only thing she could see that reminded her of the changes. Changes only she could feel.

The dress was beautiful—short but not too short, with bright, loud circles and a silky neckline that gave her goose bumps when she tried it on—but it wasn't perfect. She'd known about the torn seam when she brought it home; it was the reason the dress was so cheap. But it wasn't until that morning, the very morning of the event at the Ferry Building, when Hazel realized that unless she wanted to meet her mother with six inches of torso hanging out, she would need to have the dress fixed.

When she'd first seen the business card hanging from a thread and safety-pinned to the tag, she'd assumed it was just the name of the dress designer: MARIPOSA OF THE MISSION. But standing in front of her closet that morning, she'd looked closer. There, under the address, was a single word: SEAMSTRESS.

And that's how she ended up in the Mission on a Sunday

afternoon, standing in a dusty shop that smelled like moth-balls, crowded with sewing machines and headless dress dummies, and which was, apparently . . .

"Closed," the girl on the couch said again. "Sorry."

But she didn't sound sorry. She sounded annoyed. Which was about when Hazel decided that her "funny feeling" had been right. She'd taken four buses to get there, and would in a matter of hours be meeting the one person she'd been dreaming of meeting her entire life. She owned only one dress, a dress with a skin-baring rip up one side, a dress in desperate need of mending. And in front of her, this *seamstress,* sitting surrounded by sewing machines, in a shop dedicated to fixing dresses, was telling her the store was closed?

Hazel wanted to scream. Of course something would go wrong. Learning her mother's name may have changed every fiber of who Hazel was on the inside, but in the outside world, exactly nothing was different.

"Great," Hazel huffed, settling her plain black canvas tote closer to one shoulder. She took one last look at the strange and empty shop. Business didn't appear to be booming. "You know," she started, angry words backing up in her throat. "Keeping regular business hours might go a long way. I mean, if you ever find yourself interested in any actual customers."

Hazel spun on her heel and started to push through the door, but one of her bag's thick straps caught on a brass hook and tugged her back into the room. The dress spilled out of her tote, the satiny circles bright and cheerful against the dusty, muted floorboards.

Hazel's cheeks flushed red. *Perfect,* she thought as she bent down to stuff the dress back into her bag. *Just perfect.*

"Wait." Two clunky clogs were suddenly making their way to where Hazel was crouched by the door. "That dress," the girl said, pointing one long, spindly finger at Hazel's tote. "May I see it?"

Hazel slowly held the dress out toward the girl's open hand.

"Where did you get it?" the girl asked, spreading the material and holding it out to one side.

"In the Haight," Hazel offered. "A thrift store. I think it's part of a school or something. I guess I just liked the colors. . . ." Hazel shuffled her feet and let her voice trail off. Why was she defending her fashion sense to a grumpy girl with weird bangs who, until recently, was primarily interested in getting her to leave?

The girl was staring at her with eyes that looked more feline than human: small, piercing, and almost golden. "What do you need it for?" she asked slowly.

"I'm going to a fund-raiser," Hazel said. "It's at this restaurant in the Ferry Building. The Slanted Door?" She took another full breath, before adding, "I'm meeting my mother tonight."

It was the first time Hazel had said it—any of it—out loud, and the words felt like sharp explosions in her mouth. She looked at the tops of her checkered, slip-on sneakers.

The girl was quiet, and Hazel could tell she was still staring at her. Finally the girl turned, her heavy clogs scraping the floor, and walked slowly back to the couch. She took the dress with her. "Can you come back in two hours?"

Hazel stared at the girl's small back, the arch of her spine curving beneath her thin sweater as she laid the dress over the arm of the love seat. "Two hours?" she repeated. "Yeah—I mean, yes. Sure. Are you sure?" Hazel waited for the girl to turn back around, to say something more. When she didn't, Hazel put her hand on the doorknob, afraid that another word would make the girl change her mind.

"Hey," she heard from behind her. The girl was still standing over the couch, her back to Hazel as she spoke. "What's your name?"

"Oh, sorry." Hazel blushed. "I'm Hazel."

"Nice to meet you, Hazel," the girl said, landing heavily on each word like she was sharing a secret. "I'm Posey. See you at three."

2

I am meeting my mother tonight.

Hazel sat on a bench in Dolores Park, the after-noon sun warming the back of her neck. Her long legs were crossed and one bounced furiously over the other, her floppy bag and an enormous iced coffee clutched between both hands. It was all she could do to sit still, her mind turning over and over, centered on a single thought:

I am meeting my mother tonight.

Or at least, that's where the thinking began. From there, it traveled a fairly linear course, hitting predictable speed bumps *(But what if she isn't there? What if she doesn't want to meet me? What if she's horrible and mean?)* until ultimately circling back to where it began.

I am meeting my mother tonight.

Hazel slurped through the remaining cubes of ice and tossed the plastic cup into a nearby recycling bin. Before she knew where she was going, her feet had whisked her away.

She bolted between two lanes of traffic and started down a

...et, absentmindedly rummaging through her bag with ...e hand. Her fingers landed on a familiar hulk of black plastic, and she immediately felt her pulse leveling.

Whenever she felt anxious, or confused, or antsy, Hazel reached for her camera, a vintage Polaroid that had once belonged to Wendy. Taking pictures was less a hobby than a physical urge. Sort of the way your feet find their way out from under the covers at night when you're suddenly too hot. It was instinctual. Something she needed to do.

On the corner of Seventeenth Street was a used bookstore, with a rolling rack of sale books on display out front. Hazel walked by it twice before pausing off to one side. She crouched low on the curb and brought the boxy lens up to her right eye, snapping a quick shot of the weathered spines.

"You know, I think people usually like those things for what's *inside.*"

Hazel looked down at the long, lanky shadow cutting the sidewalk beside her. She recognized the shoes before the voice. They laced up the front and were cool in an old-school, grandpa kind of way. There was only one person she knew who could get away with wearing shoes like that.

"Jasper," she sighed, planting her hands on the ground and hoisting herself up. "You scared me."

She turned to find Jasper Greene smiling his trademarked heart-shaped grin, hands stuffed in the pockets of his faded blue jeans. Jasper was the first person Hazel had spoken to at her new school last fall. They were two of only four people who had signed up for the yearlong Mixed Media elective, and were often partnered up for projects. He was one of those rare floaters who didn't really fit into any one group at school and, as a result, was totally comfortable talking to anyone. Whether or not either of them realized it, he was probably the closest thing Hazel had found recently to a friend.

"Who, me?" Jasper gasped, taking a step back. "You're the one lurking around, all paparazzi style. Was that you jumping behind a tree when I got off the bus?"

Hazel rolled her eyes. "What are you doing here?" she asked, flapping the blurry Polaroid. She still felt jittery and wondered if it was the coffee.

"Taco truck on Harrison," Jasper said, nodding toward the end of the block. His dark, curly hair flopped over his eyes and he pushed it away. "It's a Sunday ritual. What about you?"

"Nothing," Hazel blurted out. Jasper may have been the one person she knew well enough to talk to on the street, but it didn't mean she was about to tell him her life story. "Just walking around."

"Whatcha got there?" Jasper asked, gesturing to the photo she was still shaking in one hand. Hazel flipped it over and held it up with a shrug. It was a close-up of three books side by side. Hazel had been drawn to their mishmashed typeface and fraying seams.

"Cool." Jasper smiled. "Miss Lew was totally right about you."

"Right about what?" Hazel stuffed the photo in the pocket of her sweatshirt and pulled the soft material closer to her waist. Miss Lew was their art teacher, and the person who had demanded that Hazel apply to art school in New York City for the fall. In the end, Hazel had applied, though it was Miss Lew who had filled out the forms, sent in her portfolio, and even written a check for the application fee. Hazel had been accepted just after winter break. Miss Lew was ecstatic, and Hazel had pretended to be happy, but she already knew she wasn't going. She'd never been out of the state of California, let alone all the way across the country, and what was the point of going to art school, anyway? It was silly, not to mention astronomically expensive. Taking pictures was something she did for fun, and to stay sane. She didn't need a degree for that. Much less a lifetime of loans.

"She said you were the most talented photographer she'd ever had in class," Jasper said flatly, looking Hazel squarely in the eyes. "She said you see things different than everyone else."

Hazel's skin prickled. It always gave her a jolt, hearing that other people were talking about her. Not so much that they had nice things to say, just that they had noticed her at all. Maybe it was because she moved around so much, or because she spent almost all of her time imagining her life was different. Imagining that she knew where she came from, who her parents were, what they looked like, what they did. Hazel had no idea who she really was; how was anybody else supposed to know her, either?

"I tried not to take offense," Jasper went on with a smile. "Luckily, the word on the street is that New York is a pretty big town. Think there's room for both of us?"

Jasper had gotten in early to film school at NYU. They'd worked together on a short film he'd done for his application, and he'd admitted that he'd always wished he was a better photographer. She thought the stills he'd taken on set were pretty good, but she hadn't said anything.

"Anyway," Jasper sighed dramatically, like talking to her was a challenge. Hazel had no idea why he tried so hard. "I'm about to head down to SOMA to check out this new gallery show," he said. "It's birds, I think. Or trees. Want to come?"

"Can't," Hazel said, scuffing the top of her sneaker against the rack of books. "I should get going, actually."

Jasper tilted his head to one side, a thatch of dark hair shadowing his face. "How about later on? There's supposed to be this really good Thai place near the museum."

Jasper was always telling Hazel about the best new this or some totally underrated that. She imagined he must be on every mailing list and RSS feed in cyber-town, and couldn't tell if he really wanted to hang out with her or just show off how many blogs he read.

"Can't," Hazel said again. "I have plans."

Jasper nodded. "Right. Okay." He clapped his hands and smiled again, his lips curling into a giant heart around his perfectly straight white teeth. "Tomorrow, then?"

Hazel checked her watch, a digital piece of plastic she'd won in an arcade in Santa Cruz. It was almost time to pick up her dress.

"Tomorrow?" she echoed, the tiniest hint of exasperation creeping into her voice. "Tomorrow's Monday."

"Perfect." Jasper grinned. "Get the week started right."

Hazel opened her bag and tucked her camera back inside.

"Hazel," Jasper said quietly.

"Yeah?" Hazel responded, pulling her hair out from under the strap of her bag. "Sorry, I'm just, kind of, hurrying, I have to—"

"You're going to have to give me a chance someday," Jasper said lightly, holding her gaze again.

Just like that, Hazel's cheeks were on fire. She checked her watch again, only this time she didn't see anything but a blur of skin and plastic. "Okay," she said, readjusting her bag and scurrying off down the street.

"Okay?" Jasper called after her, a laugh in his voice. "Tomorrow, then?"

Hazel tucked her hair behind her ears and prayed for the light to change so she could cross the street. After an eternity, it did. She yelled over her shoulder as she skipped to the crosswalk. "Sure, whatever."

Jasper clasped his hands over his head, like a champion boxer at the center of the ring.

"I'll take it," he called out. "See you tomorrow!"

3

*H*azel locked herself in a stall of the Ferry Building's public restroom and hung the unopened garment bag from Posey's shop on the door. She stared at its long, shadowy shape, trying to come up with reasons for leaving it zipped. Because unzipping it, she knew, would lead to trying the dress on. Trying the dress on would lead to wearing it, and once she was wearing it, she had little choice but to step out of the stall and exit the bathroom completely. And once she was outside, she knew where she'd end up. Her mother was in a restaurant less than the length of a football field away. And once she was in the same room with her mother—her mother!—she'd probably have to think of something to say.

But first, she'd have to get dressed.

Hazel ran her fingers through her hair, tugging at her auburn roots and squeezing her temples between the flats of her palms. She remembered the year she spent with Roy's sister, Rae Ann, who lived on a lake up north. Rae Ann was intent on teaching Hazel to dive, and had shouted encouragement while Hazel stood on the dock. Hazel had gripped the edge of the wooden plank with her toes and watched them turn from red to pink to white. She'd learned how to swim only a few months before and couldn't imagine anything worse than propelling herself headfirst into the cold, murky water. Everything inside of her was screaming to stop, turn around. Go back.

Eventually, she'd given up and taken the plunge. The cold shock of water stung her skin and she'd had a hard time catching her breath for a few moments afterward. But, in the end, she'd survived.

Hazel took a deep breath and unzipped the heavy gray plastic, reaching both hands inside the garment bag.

Right away, the dress felt different. Not "different" in the sense that Posey had done such amazing work that Hazel hardly recognized it. "Different" in the sense that it was a completely different dress.

Hazel sat down on the toilet seat lid. She heard a strange noise, like a gasping, or a breathy cackle, and it took her a few seconds to realize she was laughing.

Posey had given her the wrong dress! Of course she had. Of *course* Hazel would have nothing to wear. Of course she wasn't going to meet her mother tonight.

A wave of relief rolled up and over Hazel. She'd been given the gift of an excuse. An actual excuse, something that was totally and completely beyond her control.

But quickly, the wave crashed, and Hazel was left shaking her head.

Really? Her mother, her birth mother, was in the room next door, and she wasn't going to meet her? Because of somebody else's stupid mistake?

She ripped the gown from the hanger and stepped out of her jeans, leaving them in a pile on the checkered floor. She pulled the dress up to her shoulders, wriggled her arms through the sleeves, slipped her feet into the boring black flats she'd found at Goodwill the week before, and pushed her way out of the stall.

The bathroom was empty and there were mirrors on all three walls, sending Hazel's reflection back and forth, deep into layers of glass. Hazel stood in front of a row of porcelain sinks, her breath trapped in her lungs.

She turned around.

Because, although she knew it defied the law of optics, she had no choice but to assume that the reflection she was seeing, over and over again, belonged to somebody else.

The dress was stunning. She could see that now. It was a shimmery, teal green, and short, just like the other dress had been. But instead of abruptly ending at her knees, it sort of billowed out from her hips, giving her pale, slightly knock-kneed legs a shape. The neck was an easy, swooping cowl, and the delicate cap sleeves gave her usually sticklike arms the illusion of sleek contour.

But more than the way it looked, Hazel couldn't believe the way the dress felt. Usually, her clothes hung on her body uncomfortably. This dress felt like it was made especially for her, barely even touching her skin in some places and resting like a material mist in others.

Hazel twirled and watched as the skirt spun behind her. She could feel her lips cinching up in a smile, and was about to take a second spin around when she heard low voices from the other side of the bathroom door.

Hazel scooted toward the sink and turned on a faucet, just as the door swung open. A petite woman with thick, blond hair passed behind her, dressed in head-to-toe black and bouncing a little girl on her hip. The girl was maybe two or three years old, her fine hair pulled back with rhinestone daisy clips.

"Wash our hands! Wash our hands!" the little girl was shouting gleefully, clapping her fingers together and holding her chubby arms out toward the sink.

"I know, I know, Bub," the woman cooed as she flipped on the faucet with her elbow.

Hazel rubbed her own hands together under the water, trying not to stare. In the mirror, her eyes fell on the woman's necklace, a simple chain with a purple stone or shell at the center.

"She's in this water phase," the woman said without looking up, and Hazel realized she was talking to her. "I don't know what her deal is."

"My deal, my deal," the little girl sang, splashing in the running water. The woman rolled her eyes and smiled at the mirror, just as Hazel quickly turned, waving her hands beneath the automated paper towel dispenser.

Hazel collected her bag from the stall and made her way toward the door. Out of the corner of her eye, she could see the woman kneeling low to the ground, whispering sweetly as she patted the little girl's hands dry.

Normally, a scene like this made Hazel want to hit something. Without warning, her mind would instantly drift back to everything she'd lived without. All of the times she'd dried her own hands, all of the nicknames she'd never had. Her blood would burn; the veins in her forehead would start to twitch. Why should somebody else get all of the things that she never had?

But not tonight. Tonight, as the woman in black straightened the hem of her little girl's skirt, Hazel smiled.

At last, she was going to meet her mother.

4

Hazel stood outside the sleek, windowed dining room of The Slanted Door, waiting for some kind of sign.

She wasn't exactly sure what *kind* of a sign she was expecting. Maybe a Moses-like parting of the seas, where the crowd of well-heeled guests would split down the middle, creating a clear path from one side of the room to the other. A beam of light, perhaps, shining down on one woman, standing alone with arms outstretched, waiting to embrace her daughter—the daughter she'd given up but never forgotten.

What Hazel saw, instead, was a roomful of strangers gathered in a four-star restaurant. In fact, if it hadn't been for a framed announcement propped on a wooden easel by the door, it could have been any group of sophisticated diners, out for a meal on any weekend night.

Hazel caught another glimpse of her reflection in the glass, the shimmering shadow of her face staring back at her. Her hair, though still growing out, looked straight and silky, and even her choppy bangs were behaving for once. Her blue eyes, which she'd always thought were too close together, sparkled and popped against the creamy white of her skin, and her nose, which was normally too long, looked, all of a sudden, elegant. She didn't understand it, but somehow even her features had shifted. She was almost pretty.

Hazel steadied her trembling hands by clasping them together at her waist, blinked back a burning in her eyes, and took a step inside.

A low buzz of conversation filled the room, and people hovered in small groups around the sleek, brown leather booths. A buffet of fancy finger foods was set up against one wall, tiers of dumplings and tempura on shiny silver trays.

Hazel tucked her hair behind her ears and approached the unmanned hostess stand. The announcement listed the name of the foundation in a big, bold font: ARTS FOR ALL. And beneath it, a color photograph of the founder and director: Rosanna Scott.

It was a portrait-style headshot of a woman with long, thick gray hair, the kind of gray that was mostly silver. Her skin was smooth and her green eyes sparkled, her smile symmetrically perfect and bright.

For the first time in her life, Hazel was seeing a picture of her birth mother, and the first thought she had was: *Nice teeth*.

Hazel reached out and steadied her hands on the bottom of the black metal frame. She was starting to feel dizzy, and took a few deep breaths as she glanced around the room.

Where was she? What would she be doing when Hazel saw her first?

A dense crowd had gathered at the bar. Hazel took a few steps closer, and noticed that at the center of the group was an older man. He was by far the most casually dressed person in the room, wearing jeans and a navy blue button-down shirt. His salt-and-pepper hair looked uncombed and he leaned with one elbow on the bar, twirling a straw in circles against his glass.

Hazel stood with her arms stiff at her sides next to a centerpiece of tall, white lilies. At the other end of the buffet, an older woman with a short black bob was nodding as a tall, dark-skinned man with a speckled gray beard spoke.

"It's just so terrible," the man was saying. "I knew she'd been sick, but I didn't realize how sick."

Hazel folded her arms and turned away, uncomfortable eavesdropping on such an intimate exchange. But the couple was making their way down the table toward her, and the woman's voice was high-pitched and impossible to ignore.

"It all happened so fast," the woman sighed. "You know, I saw her just last month. She looked beautiful, as ever. Rosanna was so strong."

Hazel's breath caught in her throat, her heart squished against her ribs.

What all had happened so fast? And did she say *was*?

"Excuse me, dear." The woman was touching her shoulder now. "Could you pass me a plate?"

Hazel looked from the woman to the stack of plates at her elbow, white porcelain with gold stripes around the edges. With robotic movements she picked one from the top and passed it over.

"Sorry," Hazel heard herself saying. "Were you, did you just say . . . ?"

The woman stared at Hazel, her eyes warm and understanding as she touched Hazel's elbow. "Were you a friend of Rosanna's?" she asked. Behind her, the man was tilting a miniature ceramic pitcher over his plate, pouring a stream of thick, dark soy sauce onto a pile of sticky white rice.

"Um, no." Hazel's vision blurred. "Rosanna?"

The woman continued to nod like a slow-motion bobblehead.

"Yes," the woman said, selecting two pairs of chopsticks wrapped in red linen napkins. "It's wonderful that they decided to go ahead with the event. Rosanna worked so hard on it every year. And I know she would've wanted us to remember her together."

Hazel felt her eyes widening, her pulse raging in her ears. She looked around the room. Everyone was dressed in black. The somber man at the bar, receiving condolences. It wasn't a party. It was a wake.

The man dropped a heavy hand on the woman's shoulder and leaned in, whispering something about finding a table by the window. The woman smiled at Hazel and gave her elbow a final squeeze before following her companion across the room.

🦋 🦋 🦋

The ferry was just about to leave when Hazel scurried on board.

She had scrambled out of the restaurant in a haze, pushing open the double doors and shoving her way through the crowds of tourists arranging themselves into photographable poses as the sun slipped behind them and into the bay. Without thinking, she'd walked across the dock toward the boat to Marin, only remembering to buy a ticket when prompted by the indifferent attendant at the booth.

Her face was already wet with tears by the time she found a seat outside. The night air was cold and the wind whipped loose strands of hair into her stinging eyes.

Rosanna Scott was dead.

All of this time, they had been living so close, at times maybe even neighbors. For all Hazel knew, they could have ridden the same trolley. Or been stopped at the same crosswalk. Her whole life, the one person she was searching for was literally around the corner.

And now she was gone forever.

It was unfair, Hazel knew. But she was over *fair*. She didn't even know what fair was anymore. When every day finds new and exciting ways to let you down, you start to expect disappointment. But she hadn't expected it to hurt so much.

She'd never even met Rosanna. But now that she knew she never would, she felt an emptiness, sharper and deeper than anything she'd ever felt before. When Wendy had died, Hazel had been so little. Her entire relationship with her adoptive mother was a tapestry of holes, woven out of foggy memories, a handful of Roy's stories, and the knowledge that Wendy was already dead.

Even though Hazel had only known Rosanna's name for a few short months, she'd spent a lifetime imagining that her birth mother was out there, waiting to be found. Just the idea of her was a distant comfort, like the shadows of a mountain range, hugging the desert horizon. The idea that somewhere, just on the other side of those peaks, there had to be more than this.

And now that idea was dead, too.

Hazel leaned against the boat's metal railing. There was

nobody else on the deck; everyone had already found a spot inside, protected from the brisk ocean chill. Hazel couldn't feel the cold. She dropped her head in her hands and sobbed, tears tripping down the front of her hand-sewn dress.

First Wendy, then a life of being barely remembered, tossed around like an afterthought. Now this? How much more was she supposed to take?

"It isn't fair," Hazel whispered into the crook of her elbow. "I just wish I'd gotten to know her first." Hazel exhaled, a choppy hiccup, and folded her arms behind her knees. Her pulse beat like a metronome in her ears, marking time between each sniffle and sob.

At first, it felt like a tickle. An itch, just above her cheekbone.

Thinking it was a tear caught between her lashes, Hazel lifted her head and brought a hand to her face. But the tickling had stopped.

Instead, she felt a flutter on her knee, near the pattern of fallen tears where her cheek had been pressed against her dress.

Then, she spotted a little golden patch, like a tag, at the hem of her skirt, just above her knees. She lifted the material off of her skin and realized that the patch was a tiny embroidered butterfly.

Funny, she thought. She hadn't noticed anything there before.

And then something happened. She was sure she was dreaming, because it looked—and it felt—like the butterfly was moving.

Hazel brought the green-blue fabric closer to her eyes, and

sure enough, the little golden wings were flapping, the butterfly freeing itself from the silky material of her dress.

Hazel scrambled to her feet. *It must be shock,* she thought.
*This must be what people mean when they talk about grief
making you crazy.*

But just as she was beginning to breathe again, she felt
one last flutter against her kneecap, and watched with wide,
clear eyes as the glowing butterfly detached from her dress. It
flapped its delicate wings, hovering for a moment at eye level,
and then zipped out over the water, disappearing against the
sinking sun.

Hazel shook her head and slumped back down against the
railing, cradling her bag in her lap. She closed her eyes and
drifted off just as the boat pulled away from shore, the low
rumble of the engine lulling her to sleep.

5

The first thing that Hazel noticed after she woke up was that she was still on a boat. And that it was morning. Or at least the patch of sky she could see from where she was curled up against the boat's railing *looked* like morning: pale, pale blue and dusted with cloud strings. Had she really slept on the boat all night long? It must have docked overnight, but how many trips across the bay had she made while asleep?

Hazel ran her fingers through her long, stringy hair, working through tangles near the back of her neck and squeezing her eyes tightly shut. She ached all over, partially from being wedged between a column and the side of the boat's metal bars, but mostly from remembering the night before.

Scenes and faces flashed behind her closed eyes: the couple at the buffet, the little girl with daisy clips, Rosanna's picture, frozen in a frame . . .

Hazel sighed and carefully lifted herself up to shaky feet, placing her hands on the railing and looking out across the water. She was disoriented and glanced quickly over both shoulders.

Was the ferry heading to Marin, or back to San Francisco? She craned her neck in both directions, but couldn't see either one. Not the hills of Marin, with the tall, extended point of Mt. Tamalpais stretching out in the distance. And to her other side, not the port, or anything resembling the jagged formation of buildings that made up the city skyline downtown. In fact, there was no land to be seen at all. Which was pretty much impossible, since the bay between the Port of San Francisco and Marin was spotted with islands, and there was always at least one bridge visible at all times.

She scooped up her bag and slung it over her shoulder, searching the cabin of the boat for the door. But in the very spot where the door should've been, there was only a solid wall.

Hazel glanced around the unfamiliar deck, a strange whooshing sound suddenly echoing in her ears. There was no question about it. She was on a different boat.

It was similar to the boat that ran from Larkspur to the city, but about three times as big. And where the Larkspur ferry was mostly open deck with a small, rounded cabin in the middle, this boat was boxy and completely covered, except for a narrow walkway around the perimeter.

How had she not noticed last night?

Hazel scanned the deck for somebody in an official-looking uniform, hoping to find the boat's captain. The crisp spray from the ocean misted the tops of her cheeks. Out in the distance, the shadow of land was sharpening into view. There was still no skyline, no port. Only rolling dunes and a cluster of white-shingled houses.

Where the hell was she? And how was she ever going to get home?

Hazel was about to start back around the other side of the boat when she heard a crackling overhead. She looked up to find a small loudspeaker wedged above a window, and moved toward it.

"Ladies and gentlemen, this is your captain speaking," a gruff male voice boomed through the speaker. He had some kind of accent that Hazel recognized but couldn't place right away. "In just a few minutes we'll be arrivin' in Oak Bluffs."

Oak Bluffs? Hazel had never heard of it. Was she north or south of Marin?

"Drivahs, please return to your vehicles; all walk-off passen-jahs, please make your way to the stah-board side of the ship."

It was a Boston accent, Hazel realized with shock.

"Thank you and welcome to Mahtha's Vin-yahd."

Static hissed through the loudspeaker before the micro-phone clicked off. Hazel stared at it dumbly, swaying back and forth against the big, rounded window.

Martha's Vineyard?

She wasn't sure exactly where that was, but for some reason, all she could think of was tennis courts and presidents. Wasn't Martha's Vineyard where rich people went on vacation?

And wasn't it on the East Coast?

Hazel turned back toward the water. The harbor was inch-ing closer and she saw that it was dotted with sailboats. At the center, a rickety old wooden dock was lined with rows of cars, waiting to drive onto the next boat.

A crowd had gathered at the top of a narrow staircase. *Must be stah-board,* Hazel thought, and opened the door to wait in line. Wherever she was, she couldn't stay on a boat forever.

Hazel stood at the back of the line, behind two older men in paint-stained T-shirts and black rubber boots. One of them was reading a newspaper. Hazel peeked over his shoulder to see the masthead at the top.

It was the *Boston Globe*.

The line inched farther down the stairs and Hazel stepped aside, slumping on the top step with her back to the wall. She stared blankly ahead at the squares of chipped white paint on the wall. She took a deep breath and exhaled slowly.

I must be dreaming, Hazel thought, and closed her eyes. *This has to be some kind of nightmare, the kind where you realize you're dreaming but still can't wake up.*

Wake up, Hazel silently implored. *Wake up, wake up, wake up.*

She squeezed one eye open, her stomach flip-flopping at the sight of the unmoved wall. She scooped her bag into her lap, wincing as it landed with a graceless thud. Had it always been this heavy?

Hazel reached inside the tote, automatically feeling around for her camera. Her hand quickly cupped the square lens and she breathed a sigh of relief. Next to the camera was the plastic garment bag from Posey's shop. She remembered crumpling it up and stuffing it inside in the Ferry Building bathroom the night before. Only now, the bag didn't feel crumpled.

Or empty.

Hazel pulled the bag free from her tote and laid it out across her lap. She tugged down the zipper and a handwritten note fluttered out. It was stapled twice to the back of a business card, identical to the one Hazel had found on the

thrift store dress. MARIPOSA OF THE MISSION. She freed the
note from the card and unfolded it.

Dear Hazel,

*As you've probably figured out, the dress I
gave you was not the dress you brought to me. It
was a dress made especially with you in mind, and
it had the power to grant you one wish.*

*Which, if you're reading this, you've already
made.*

*In this bag you will find two other dresses,
each with the same wish-granting power.*

Here are the rules:

No talking about wishes. *(This is for your own
good. Nothing says "crazy" like a girl who thinks
she wears magical clothing.)*

One dress, one wish. *(And once you've already
wished on a dress, it's just a dress.)*

No repeat wishes. *(Bo-ring.)*

No wishing on behalf of the universe. *(I'd like
to feed the hungry, too, but it's not that kind of
magic.)*

No wishing for more wishes. *(Duh.)*

*Finally, these wishes have been given to you
because you deserve them. So wish carefully and
wish from your heart. Those are the only wishes
that count.*

> *Best wishes!*
> *(Sorry . . . had to.)*
> *Posey*

35

Hazel looked down at the note in her hands, which had started to tremble. A wish? *What wish?*

The note fell to the step below hers, and as she bent to pick it up, she noticed a small, golden graphic on the other side.

It was the same butterfly she'd seen the night before, flying out of her dress and into the night sky. The butterfly she'd thought she'd imagined.

Hazel closed her eyes again and leaned her head back against the stairwell, forcing herself to return to that moment in the dark. She'd been thinking about Rosanna. She'd said some words out loud. But what had she . . .

Suddenly, Hazel bolted to her feet, nearly knocking into the man with the newspaper.

I wish I had gotten to know her first.

Rosanna. She'd wished she'd gotten to know Rosanna. Could that have something to do with why she had woken up on a boat she'd never seen before, three thousand miles from home?

It didn't make any sense. Rosanna was dead. How would sending Hazel to Martha's Vineyard bring her mother back?

Loud, mechanical noises came from below, and Hazel lurched forward as the boat scuttled against the dock. At the bottom of the staircase, the heavy metal door creaked open and a square of bright morning sun filtered through. A bearded man in a vest stood off to the side, ushering the eager crowd out onto the rickety wooden plank. The line shifted and Hazel took the stairs carefully. Just as she reached the lower deck, the man in rubber boots folded his newspaper in half and tossed it aside. The paper landed on a low table between one of the leather booths, the black and gray print popping out against the glossy red Formica.

Hazel picked up the paper to bring the small print closer. Her eyes blurred over the flowery script until suddenly, everything disappeared but the date:

Monday, June 29th.

And the year . : . not this year. . . .

But eighteen years in the past.

Hazel felt the paper slipping from her fingers as her knees buckled, folding her body in half over the unforgiving edges of the booth.

Posey had said that she'd made a wish come true. But she hadn't mentioned that Hazel would need to go back in time to do it.

And not just back to any time . . .

Back to the year she was born.

6

azel stood frozen at the end of the dock. She'd been swept along by the bustling crowd, as the line of passengers shuffled off of the boat and down a metal ramp. A covered wooden dock fed them out to the road, where an impatient traffic cop was furiously waving one arm, ushering them across the newly painted crosswalk.

"Any day now, Princess."

Hazel snapped out of her trance to see that she was the only person left on the curb. She wanted to move, but she couldn't. Posey's note was crumpled in her hand and she gripped it with all of her strength, as if it were the only thing keeping her anchored to the ground.

Breathe, Hazel commanded herself. *Just keep breathing.*

She turned to look behind her at the boat, the wide doors open like a giant mouth, gobbling up the rows of cars and passengers waiting to make the return trip. She knew it wouldn't take her back to California, but still, part of her wanted to climb back on board.

Breathe, she reminded herself again. She locked eyes with the traffic cop, who was shooting her an exhausted stare and tapping one foot against the pavement. She had no idea where she was supposed to go, but she couldn't stand on the curb forever.

As Hazel followed the paved sidewalk into town, she allowed herself a few sideways glances. To her left was a sprawling lawn, surrounded by colorful Victorian houses. To her right, a row of boardinghouses stretched out along the water, their painted NO VACANCY signs swinging in the lazy breeze.

She made her way past racks of postcards and personalized key chains, boarded-up clam shacks, and pizza joints filling the air with the heavy aroma of hot grease. Ahead, a neon sign blinked GAME ROOM, and the clang and clatter of a pinball machine escaped through the second-story windows.

Hazel walked until the sidewalk ended abruptly in front of a shingled building shaped like an old-time circus tent. Tinny music spilled out onto the street, and through slanted windows Hazel could see the blur of a merry-go-round. The circus music seemed suddenly ominous and Hazel realized that she was afraid. What was this place? How did she get here? And what was she supposed to do now?

She didn't even know what time it was. Her watch had been blinking horizontal lines since she'd woken up on the boat. It felt like late morning, but who knew what late morning felt like on Martha's Vineyard?

Eighteen years in the past.

Dull hunger pains tugged at Hazel's stomach and the familiar sensation was almost a comfort. She hadn't eaten anything since lunch the day before. Relieved to have some kind of a plan, Hazel turned away from the docks and glanced toward one of the bustling side streets. Her eyes landed on a block-lettered sign: MARTHA'S CUPS 'N' CONES.

It was early for ice cream, but it looked to be her only option. And after all she'd been through so far, ice cream for breakfast would hardly be the strangest part of her day.

Hazel took a deep breath, entering the crowded shop. A glass cooler of every flavor of ice cream imaginable ran along one side of the room, covered with tubs of colorful toppings. On the walls, cartoon drawings advertised sizes and prices, and special sundaes with names like "Oinkers Delight." The sweet, cloying smell of home-baked waffle cones and fresh-churned cream filled the air.

A rowdy group of camp kids in matching orange T-shirts tossed balled-up napkins across a long, messy table. They looked to be about eight or nine . . . which meant that in the future, they'd be that much older than Hazel herself. The idea made Hazel's stomach drop. She wondered if anybody noticed her. Could they tell that she was different? Could they even see her at all?

A woman hurried past, her blond hair pulled back in a sleek, high ponytail. She pushed a pair of strawberry-blond twin girls in a stroller, their wispy curls damp in the heat. As they made their way to the door, one of the girls stretched out a sticky hand, grabbing on to Hazel's dress and giving it a playful tug.

"Violet!" the woman scolded, brushing the girl's hand away and turning to Hazel with an embarrassed shrug. "I'm so sorry. She has this thing for dresses."

Hazel managed a smile and watched as the woman squeezed the carriage through the door. She looked down at the tiny vanilla fingerprints left on her dress. They were real, and so was she.

"What are you having?" a short girl barked at her from the other side of the counter. Hazel stared dumbly at the girl, whose chocolate brown hair had been pulled back in a messy bun and stabbed through the side with a bright yellow pencil. "Hello?" the girl tried again, louder. "Can I help you?"

"Um, sure." Hazel tried to answer, but she hadn't said anything in a while and the words got stuck in the dry tunnel of her throat. The options were overwhelming and the anxiety of ordering on the spot had weakened her appetite. "Do you have iced tea?"

The girl with the pencil bun stared at Hazel for a long moment before rolling her dark eyes and retrieving a paper cup from a stack on the counter. She slid it over the counter and gestured with her elbow toward the door. "Soda fountain's behind you," she grunted. "Eighty-nine cents."

Hazel fumbled around the inside of her tote, ducking her head between the straps for a better look. Her wallet had to be in there somewhere. But all she felt was her camera, the crinkling plastic of the garment bag, and lots of empty space.

Behind her, the line was growing impatient, and she shrunk from the glare of ten pairs of eyes, burning holes into the back of her head.

"Sorry," she stammered to the girl across the counter. "I guess I lost my wallet."

The girl snatched the cup back across the glass and tipped it upside down on the pile. "Bummer," she deadpanned, before turning to the next person in line.

Hazel clenched her teeth, her pulse pounding in her ears.

She spun around but was stuck between the glass and the broad shoulders of a boy standing behind her.

"I got it," a deep voice interjected. Hazel looked up to see a strong, tanned arm reaching out toward the counter. A crumpled dollar bill fell onto the glass and the pencil girl looked up with an irritated sigh.

"Well, if it isn't Prince Charming," the girl huffed, slipping the bill inside the register and slamming the drawer shut with her hip. The boy held out his hand and she slapped the plastic cup against it. "Next!"

Hazel felt herself being shoved out of line, her face flushing hot. "Prince Charming" was still hovering at her side and she could hardly bring herself to look up. He had the sturdy voice and solid posture of somebody who was good-looking and knew it.

"Here you go," he said, handing Hazel the plastic cup. She finally glanced up and saw that he had shaggy brown hair and warm brown eyes, with two deep dimples cut like stars between the strong lines of his cheekbones and jaw.

Good-looking was an understatement.

"Thanks," Hazel muttered, following him through the crowd to a soda fountain at the back of the room. "You didn't have to do that. I have my wallet, somewhere."

"No worries." He shrugged. "Happens to the best of us."

He stood to the side of the soda fountain and reached back for Hazel's cup.

"I can do it," she insisted, angling her cup against the ice paddle. Tiny pebbles of frost sputtered down on her wrist. Her cheeks were on fire. Already, she was a charity case.

"This thing's pretty temperamental," the boy offered. He

slapped the ancient-looking machine hard on one side until it coughed up three or four perfectly formed squares of ice. He smiled, the two starry dimples burrowing deeper into his cheeks. "Sometimes it just needs a little extra love."

The boy slid into a booth beneath a bulletin board that was plastered with hand-drawn announcements. He gestured for her to sit, and Hazel perched tentatively at the edge of the plastic bench. Sitting seemed easier than coming up with a reason not to. She stared at a trail of crumbs on the tabletop, gripping the cup between her hands.

"That's a nice dress," the boy said, and Hazel immediately regretted her decision to join him. The only thing worse than being pitied was being mocked. She glanced sideways at the boy's face, prepared to snap back and walk away.

But something wouldn't let her. He was staring right at her, but there wasn't anything intimidating in his deep brown eyes. No pity, no making fun. He looked like he'd meant what he said. Like conversation was something he enjoyed.

"Is this your first time on the island?" he went on, leaning back comfortably into the sticky red leather. "You kind of have that deer-in-the-headlights, I-still-can't-believe-I'm-on-vacation sort of look."

Hazel smiled in spite of herself. If he only knew.

"Not that it's a bad thing," he backtracked. "I just see it every summer. You get a kind of radar after a while. You know?"

"Sure." She nodded and hoped it was convincing.

"So?" he asked. "Where are you from? I'm Luke, by the way."

Hazel took a long sip of sticky-sweet iced tea and gulped

it down. "Hazel," she introduced herself. "Hazel Snow. I'm from—"

Hazel was just settling into the comfortable rhythm of her own voice, and momentarily forgetting to be freaked out, when something caught her eye from behind Luke's shoulder. It was a glossy, color ad on the bulletin board, and in the mess of hand-scrawled notes from babysitters in search of babies and renters looking for rooms, it stuck out like a sore, professionally printed thumb. Hazel's eyes had quickly scanned the printed text and jumped to a name, indented at the bottom: CONTACT: ROSANNA SCOTT.

Hazel lurched across the table, barely registering how close her shoulder came to bumping against Luke's. She grabbed for one of the perforated rectangles, which displayed Rosanna's name again, this time next to a phone number.

She was still stretched long over the booth, staring numbly at the paper in her hands, when she heard Luke laugh.

"If I'd known you needed a job that bad, I would've bought you some ice cream, too." He smiled and slouched toward the window.

Hazel slid back to her side of the booth, the tiny piece of paper already dampening between the tips of her fingers. "What?" she asked, not fully registering what he'd said. She looked back at the poster on the board and this time saw the bold lettering at the top.

LOOKING FOR HOUSEHOLD HELP! the sign announced. It seemed to be an ad for a caretaking job.

"Oh, no, I just—" Hazel started to explain but stopped. What else could she possibly say?

"I mean, yes. I need a job," she said firmly, suddenly.

"Why? Do you know this place?" Hazel flattened the square of paper on the table, Rosanna's name staring back up at them. Luke glanced down at it, the star-shaped dimples springing back into place.

"Yeah," he said, clearing his throat. "You could say that."

Hazel looked back at the paper, the little printed words swimming in her vision. Her heart was a buoy, bobbing in her chest, and she couldn't believe her good luck.

"You do?" she asked quickly. "Do you know how to get there?"

Luke glanced out the window, squinting and biting the corner of his lip. "I'd give you a ride, but I walked to town," he said. "There's a free shuttle bus that stops across the street from the merry-go-round. Take it all the way into Chilmark and tell the driver to drop you off at the General Store. There's a trail on the left. Walk all the way down to the water, and you'll see it. It's pretty hard to miss."

Hazel was halfway to the door when he'd finished giving directions. She only remembered to thank him when she was out on the street.

She turned to see Luke leaning against the glass, one hand raised in a tentative wave. "Thanks!" she called out to the window, before racing off toward the bus.

Hazel felt a tiny tug between her ribs and quickly wondered if she'd ever see him again, this Prince Charming who'd swooped in and saved her day. But the wrinkled paper in her hand reminded her of why she was here. She was about to find what she was looking for.

Her mother was only a bus ride away.

7

"Here you go."

After clattering for what felt like miles down a long, bumpy dirt road, the shuttle bus slowed to a stop. The driver, a cheerful man in a floppy red visor, pulled the door open and Hazel stepped onto a gravel trail.

"Follow the path," the driver urged, pointing over Hazel's shoulder toward an expanse of lawn and sky. Just beyond the peaks of a tall, green cliff, she saw the ocean, deep blue and dotted with rolling whitecaps. "If you end up underwater, you've gone too far."

Hazel thanked him and stood in place as the van rolled back over the gravel driveway. She started down the path, her feet crunching over the layers of crumbled seashells, jagged and fine with hints of pale purple inside.

The house was one low level sprawled out across the lawn. Covered, open-air walkways connected different sections, and rounded cupolas peeked out of the white cedar-shingled roof. Hazel stood at the entrance and peeled the now-sticky material of her dress away from her body. She took a deep breath.

She was about to knock when she heard a noise behind her. It sounded like a screen door swinging shut. As she listened harder, sounds of soft, classical music wafted past, punctuated by the rolling rhythm of the waves in the distance.

Hazel stepped back onto the path and followed the melodic strains of violins. The smell of fresh-cut grass mingled with the salty sea air, and Hazel gaped at the rolling hills, the manicured gardens, the open view of soft, gentle surf. At the edge of a cliff, she spotted a cozy wooden cottage, and headed for it.

A sharp pang tightened around her heart. It was the most beautiful place Hazel had ever seen. And it could have been home. It *should* have been home. If only her mother hadn't given her away.

The screen door to the cottage was stuck slightly open, and Hazel peered inside. It was just one room, with dark wood panels and a giant circular window, cut in the shape of a captain's wheel and overlooking the horizon. The walls were covered with colorful canvases, some framed, some half-finished, with many more crowded together and propped up against one another on the floor.

A woman stood in the far corner of the room, at an easel by the window. She was tall and thin, with broad shoulders and long, dark blond hair that cascaded in waves down her back. Her arms were folded at her waist and she rocked back gently on her heels, staring at the empty canvas as if waiting for it to tell her where to begin.

Hazel stood on the other side of the screen door, tiny ripples of excitement chasing away any negative thoughts. Even if she hadn't seen Rosanna's photograph, she would have known this was the woman she had spent her whole life waiting to meet. Something about just being near her made Hazel feel warm and full, and she was afraid to speak. She was afraid to do anything that would make this feeling go away.

"I can hear you breathing, Buster," Rosanna said without turning around. Hazel took a deep breath and readied herself to speak. But then Rosanna turned, her sharp brow relaxing as she noticed Hazel by the door.

"Oh my God, I thought you were the dog," Rosanna laughed, dropping a paintbrush into a can and holding out one arm toward the door. She wore an oversize, honey-colored sweater that hung down from her arm like a wing, and dark, crisp jeans, folded twice just above the tanned tops of her bare feet.

"Come in," she added, smiling, and Hazel immediately recognized the perfect row of sparkling white teeth. "Can I help you?"

Hazel pulled the screen door open and took a careful step inside. "Hi," she said, tucking her hair behind one ear. "I was just—I saw your ad. In town? And . . ."

"Of course." Rosanna nodded and wrapped the loose ends of her sweater around her slender waist, taking a few steps toward Hazel. "That would be Billy, my husband. He went a little crazy with the posters this year. I swear I think I even saw one in the bathroom at the vet." Rosanna laughed, a short, robust chuckle that shook her shoulders. A section of her thick, silky hair tumbled past her chin.

Hazel was trying to pay attention, but it was all she could

do to remember to blink. Standing less than three feet away from her was her biological mother. The woman whose name was on her birth certificate. The woman she'd whispered good night to every night in the dark, wondering what she was doing at that very moment, wondering if they looked alike.

Did they? Hazel wondered now. Would her own hair, despite being fine and stringy today, someday be that full and long? And though Rosanna's eyes were darker and closer to green than Hazel's blue, were they the same shape? They definitely had the same tall, lanky build, though where Hazel felt gangly and awkward, Rosanna stood confident and proud.

"Is this your first summer on the island?"

Hazel blinked and recognized the look of a question on Rosanna's face.

"Yes," Hazel managed, hugging her elbows in front of her chest. "I, I live in California. . . ."

The words tumbled out before she had decided they were the ones she wanted to say.

"So do we!" Rosanna exclaimed, laying a hand on Hazel's shoulder. Her touch was soft and gentle and sent tingles down Hazel's arm. "Well, half the year," Rosanna continued. "The half we're not here. Billy teaches computer science at Stanford. This farm has been in his family for generations and we come back every summer to keep it running. I'm an artist. . . ."

She rolled her eyes, gesturing to the canvases. "Obviously," she laughed. "And I teach, too. In Marin County, not far from San Francisco."

Hazel tried to keep her features steady, but her head was still spinning. Rosanna taught in Marin, which explained how

Hazel had been given up for adoption in San Francisco, and not in Massachusetts. Her eyes traveled to Rosanna's slim midriff. It was the end of June. If Hazel was to be born in December, she'd have to be growing inside of Rosanna by now. The idea made Hazel wince and she glanced quickly up at the paintings on the wall.

"I have a few shows coming up," Rosanna said. The pastel colors of landscapes and thoughtful portraits of people in various natural settings swirled in Hazel's view. "That's part of what I need help with, actually. In addition to keeping track of things around the house. We have a wonderful year-round caretaker, and there's a young couple that helps with the farm, but there's always so much to do. It's going to be a busy season, lots of . . . changes, I think."

Hazel looked back at Rosanna, who was now pacing the room. She lifted a curtain and peeked outside as if distracted by something she'd seen on the lawn. "Do you have any gallery experience?" she asked, a faraway look in her eyes.

"Gallery?" Hazel repeated, her mind still stuck on the word *changes*. What kind of changes? Did Rosanna already know she was pregnant? "No," Hazel answered distractedly. "I mean, not really, but—"

"Not that this is much of a gallery, no, but it would be great to have someone around to help me set up, maybe work with me to choose the pieces. . . ." Rosanna turned and studied Hazel with a smile, quickly taking in her dress. "You look like you have good taste."

Hazel blushed. "Oh, well, I don't know. . . ." She drifted off, feeling Rosanna's watchful eyes on the top of her head. This was her chance to spend time with her mother. She wasn't about to blow it by being modest. "I could learn," she said firmly, meeting Rosanna's gaze head-on.

"Fantastic." Rosanna smiled. "Do you have somewhere to stay? Are you here with family?"

Hazel shook her head quickly and looked down at the cherrywood floor. The absurdity of the situation suddenly slammed down around her. She didn't know a single person on the island, and she had not a penny to her name. What was she thinking? What was *Posey* thinking, sending her across the country with no explanation, no contacts, and no money?

"No," she finally managed. "My parents are traveling. In Europe. I'm here by myself."

Hazel held her breath, terrified to move or look up. It was the first time she'd said the words *my parents* out loud in all of her life, and as they'd tripped awkwardly out of her mouth, she felt like they might set off some kind of authenticity alarm. *False! Not possible! Doesn't exist!*

But if an alarm had gone off, only Hazel could hear it. Rosanna simply shrugged. "Not a problem," she insisted, noting Hazel's hesitation and taking her gently by the arm. "There's plenty of room in the guesthouse. Nothing fancy, but Jaime—our caretaker—has really made it her own. You can stay there, and we'll give you a small stipend in addition to room and board."

Rosanna walked through the screen door, cupping her hands around her mouth and whistling at the woods. Moments later, a hefty black lab bounded through a cluster of trees and landed at their feet, panting and pawing at the grass.

"Buster, meet—" Rosanna stopped on the lawn and turned suddenly to Hazel. "I didn't even ask your name! Typical, Rosanna," she laughed, admonishing herself.

"That's okay." She smiled. "It's Hazel."

Rosanna nodded approvingly and linked her arm with Hazel's elbow. They walked along the path beside the house, the steady surge of the waves rolling against the sand beneath them.

"Well, Hazel," Rosanna said, their feet falling into comfortable, synchronized steps. She gestured broadly around them with one long arm. "Welcome home."

8

*H*azel sat on her new bed, in her new room, with paper bags full of new clothes at her feet.

She was supposed to be unpacking. The story she'd told Rosanna about the airline losing her luggage had sounded almost true, and Hazel couldn't believe how quickly she had an entirely new wardrobe at her disposal. Not just any wardrobe, either: piles and piles of gently worn jeans and soft cotton tops, all of which Rosanna had insisted she'd been meaning to get rid of, anyway.

Hazel emptied one bag on the bed and picked through a mound of comfy-looking sweaters. Each one of them was something Rosanna had worn. They were hand-me-downs from her mother. For the first time in her life, Hazel had hand-me-downs.

And for the first time that she remembered, she had a mother.

Hazel smiled, her heart full as she looked through the tall bedroom window. The guesthouse was a small but artfully crafted cabin, perched at the top of the hill and overlooking the garden. The roof was pitched with dark wooden beams, and thick white panels were squeezed together like a jigsaw puzzle on the walls. Rosanna had given Hazel a quick tour of the kitchen and den downstairs, insisting that she help herself to whatever was in the fridge. Hazel had watched through the open screen door as Rosanna walked back across the lawn to the studio, still not quite believing that any of it was real.

Now Hazel looked up from the sweaters on her bed. The cabin had only one bedroom, which Hazel would be sharing with the caretaker. Rosanna hadn't said much about her new roommate, except that she had a day job in town, and would be arriving home any minute.

The room hardly looked lived in at all. There were no pictures in frames, no posters on the walls. Hazel quietly opened and closed a few of the top dresser drawers, eyeing neatly folded T-shirts next to careful piles of shorts and pants. Even the closet, where Hazel had carefully hung Posey's dresses, looked straight out of a hotel. Most of the hangers were empty, except for a bathrobe and a single, white sundress, pushed all the way against the wall at one end.

The only personal touch was a colorful patchwork quilt, neatly folded at the foot of the other twin bed. Hazel stood at the end of the bed and touched it, the faded fabric soft and well-worn between her fingers.

"Do you mind?"

Hazel jumped and turned to see a small girl standing in the doorway. She had long, dark hair that tumbled past her shoulders, and small, deep-set eyes that were narrowed to angry slits. If there hadn't been a pencil in her mouth, Hazel probably wouldn't have recognized her right away.

"Rule number one," the girl muttered. She took the pencil from her mouth and pushed past Hazel, ripping the quilt out of her hand. "My stuff is *my stuff*. Not *your stuff*. That means don't touch it."

Hazel stepped back, the soft part of her calves knocking into the frame of her bed. She sank heavily back onto the mattress and watched as the girl refolded the blanket with sharp, directed movements. She couldn't have been over five feet tall, and Hazel wondered how so much mean could live inside such a tiny person.

"Sorry," Hazel muttered, once she realized the girl wasn't going to say anything else. "I'm—I'm Hazel, I'm—"

"Iced tea. I remember," the girl snapped as she went to the closet and pulled a folded towel down from a high shelf. "I'm Jaime."

Hazel glanced away just as Jaime started pulling off her Cups 'N' Cones T-shirt. "I can't believe this," Jaime said, as if to herself. "Rosanna's always saying she's going to hire somebody else but she never actually *does* it."

Out of the corner of her eyes, Hazel saw Jaime wriggling out of her knee-length cutoffs and wrapping herself in the towel. "So what's your story?" Jaime asked. "Runaway? You don't look homeless."

Hazel bit the inside of her cheek and felt her eyebrows inching together. "Homeless?" she repeated, her voice sturdy and defensive. "What makes you think I'm homeless?"

Hazel hated girls like this. At the four different high schools she'd so far had the privilege of attending, she had met many of them: the tough, little girls who projected quiet disdain and had a clever comeback for everything, always. In fact, she herself had been mistaken for one of them fairly regularly. But it was Hazel's firm belief that anyone who *actually was* that unhappy usually tried a lot harder to hide it.

"Rosanna only takes in kids who need fixing," Jaime announced to a tall chest of drawers. She pulled out a pair of white sport socks and some blue cotton underwear and balled them up in her hand.

Hazel shifted on the bed, the mattress creaking heavily beneath her.

"Fine, don't tell me," Jaime sighed, shutting the drawer with a thud. "Guess we'll have plenty of time for secrets. You don't snore, do you?" Jaime paused at the door and turned to Hazel, her steely eyes cold and focused.

"No," Hazel coolly replied. The idea of she and Jaime trading secrets was almost enough to make her laugh. "Do you?"

One corner of Jaime's mouth turned up in a half-smile as she turned toward the hall. "I'll give you the grand tour when I get out," she called out from the bathroom. The spray of the water hit the shower curtain, quickly muffling as Jaime slammed the door shut.

Hazel rubbed her forehead and sighed, turning back to the pile of new clothes on her bed. She knew she should keep unpacking, but her eyes stung and her body ached. She swung her legs around the bag and curled up against the wall, glancing out the window at the main house across the lawn. Soft yellow light spilled out of the windows and Hazel tried to picture Rosanna inside.

She let her mind wander, imagining what it would be like

to stay in the main house, instead of out here with Jaime, who seemed intent on making their time together as uncomfortable as possible. But Hazel wasn't here to make friends, she reminded herself. She was here to know her mother.

Hazel felt her eyelids growing heavy and she rolled over, wisps of her half-dyed hair falling over her face. It wouldn't hurt to rest for a minute, just until Jaime got out of the shower. Just a minute, and maybe they could start over. Maybe after a shower and a quick little nap, everything would look different.

9

"Rise and shine, Slumberella."

Hazel blinked her eyes open as Jaime threw back the curtains, flooding the room with dusty sunlight. Hazel rolled over to face the wall. There was a faint thumping at the back of her head and it took her a few moments of staring at the knotted wood panels to remember where she was.

"Since you slept through your tour, I guess we'll have to do it now." Jaime was standing at the foot of Hazel's bed, twisting a handful of coarse dark hair and stabbing it with yesterday's pencil.

Hazel looked down to see that she was still wearing Rosanna's yellow shirt and jeans. She pushed herself up on her elbows and blinked as Jaime pulled a sweatshirt out of the bottom dresser drawer. Even though it was late June, Hazel could feel an early morning chill slipping in through the window. "What time is it?" she mumbled, checking the corners of her mouth for drool.

"This isn't vacation, Blondie," Jaime spat, tugging up the zipper on her navy blue sweatshirt and making her way toward the door. "You're in my world now, and sleeping in is *not* on the agenda. Meet me downstairs in five."

Jaime flashed Hazel a fake smile and pulled the door shut.

Hazel flopped back on the bed. Less than twenty-four hours ago, she had been walking around San Francisco, where everything was familiar and things made sense. Now she was in a different place, in a different time, sharing a room with a girl who made *different* seem like something to shoot for.

Hazel flung back the sheets and pulled on another pair of Rosanna's jeans and a well-worn button-down shirt. The material was soft on her skin and smelled faintly of suntan lotion. Hazel buried her face in the collar, breathing in her mother's scent as deeply as she could. In the bathroom, she splashed some water on her face and glanced at her reflection in the mirror. Out of habit, she looked up to the corner where she kept the photo of Wendy at home, and found herself wondering what Roy was doing now. Would he be worried yet? Had he even noticed she was gone?

Hazel dried her hands on a towel and hurried down the stairs. Jaime had been sitting on the porch steps, but started out across the lawn as soon as Hazel reached the door.

Hazel skipped to keep up. The property looked even more pristine than it had the day before, green and lush and practically vibrating in the sun. The air was sweet and cool, and the grass was damp with dew.

She followed Jaime up to the main house and through the sturdy front door. Inside, the house was elegant but understated. An antique chandelier greeted them in the grand foyer, and Hazel glanced across the open living room, all white furniture with a massive stone hearth, to a wall of windows, overlooking the expanse of ocean and sky.

At the end of a narrow hallway, a door opened, and a man started toward them.

"Morning, Jaime," he said. His cinnamon-colored hair was tousled and he had the focused and half-dazed look of somebody who'd been staring at a computer screen for hours on end.

"Hi, Billy," Jaime said, stepping aside to let him pass through the hall. "This is Hazel," she added reluctantly. "She works here now, I guess."

Jaime turned and walked down the main hall, leaving Hazel alone with Billy in the foyer. Billy stuck out his hand and Hazel shook it, barely able to look him in the eye. A hollowness had already settled in the pit of her stomach. It was the man from the Ferry Building event. The man standing by himself at the bar, staring sadly into his drink. All at once, Hazel remembered why he was there. He'd lost his wife. In the future, Rosanna was dead.

"Nice to meet you, Hazel." Billy smiled. His features were small and precise and looked a little bit lost in the broad expanse of his face.

"You . . . you, too," Hazel stuttered. She stood dumbstruck, staring at the man who would eventually be her father. She searched for hints of similarities. His eyes were blue, like hers, but his nose was smaller and turned up at the end.

"I'm waiting," Jaime called impatiently from somewhere at the end of the hall.

"You'd better hop to," Billy whispered, leaning in. "Don't worry. Her bite's not half as bad as her bark."

Billy winked at Hazel and continued into the living room, whistling to himself as he picked up a newspaper from a glass end table by the couch.

Hazel felt her heart swell and turned to find Jaime. She had a dad. A real dad, who did classic dad things, like whistle and read the paper.

She hurried after Jaime into the kitchen, a gigantic room with walls of windows and clear ocean views. Big industrial lamps hung from the ceiling and a long, marble island split the room in half. The stainless steel refrigerator was open and a man in white pants and a black apron was crouching low and peering inside.

"Emmett makes muffins every morning," Jaime said, pointing to a basket on the counter. "Hope you're not watching your weight."

The man at the refrigerator stood upright and turned around. He was small and trim, and if it weren't for the sharp lines around his clear green eyes Hazel would've thought he was her age.

"Who do we have here?" Emmett asked, his smile bright and mischievous as the words tumbled quickly out of his mouth, the lyrical lilt of an Irish accent rolling them into a song. "Another one for the kitchen, is it? She's pretty enough, yeah. I'll keep her."

Jaime selected a muffin from the basket and peeled down the paper wrapper. "I wish," Jaime sighed. "Unfortunately, Rosanna thinks it's me who needs help."

Emmett grinned. "Probably because you're always off gallivanting with your little boyfriend," he said with an innocent shrug.

Jaime raised the muffin in her hand as if to throw it across the room, and Emmett pretended to take cover behind the blender.

"Speaking of gallivanting," Emmett squeaked from his hiding place. "Are we on for the bonfire again tonight? I've got the marshmallows all ready for your beloved s'mores."

Hazel saw Jaime toss Emmett a sharp, warning glare. "Come on, Blondie," Jaime said as she pulled open the sliding glass door.

Hazel bit the side of her cheek and tried not to look annoyed. Apparently the bonfire was an invitation-only event.

"You ever need a break from her highness, you just come see me," Emmett said as Hazel passed, and she forced a smile. She had a feeling she'd be taking him up on that offer, and soon.

Jaime was halfway across the stone patio, on the other side of a long, glass table, when Hazel caught up. "Where's Rosanna?" Hazel asked—she hoped casually—as they passed the empty studio. "When does she do her painting?"

Jaime led them into a clearing in the woods, where the trail of seashells ended and a rambling dirt path began. "Whenever she feels like it," she muttered, pushing a few spindly branches out of her way. One snapped back and nearly caught Hazel across the face. She ducked quickly and walked hunched over until they were officially out of the woods.

At the end of the path, a hulking red barn asserted itself against the clear blue sky. The oversize front doors were pulled open, revealing two rows of horse stalls and an indoor-outdoor pen, where a dozen sheep and goats were quietly grazing.

"Listen," Jaime said, and stopped short. "I know Rosanna said you'd be helping her out some in the studio, and believe me, I have no problem with that. But as long as you're with me, your business is *here*." Jaime pointed emphatically at the barn. "Got it?"

Hazel swallowed. Had she really traveled back in time just to play farmhand to some grumpy little brat?

But this was what Rosanna had told her to do. For now, she had no choice. And being close to her mother would make it all worthwhile in the end.

"Got it," she mumbled to Jaime's back as she followed her into the barn.

The smell of manure and dry hay stung Hazel's nostrils. The closest she'd ever come to farm animals was the chicken coop at Roy's sister's lake house. She had been in charge of feeding them in the mornings and, after an unfortunate incident with a disgruntled laying hen, suffered nightmares of being pecked to pieces for weeks. Now she eyed the cranky-looking goats with suspicion as Jaime took a quick turn and started up a narrow staircase inside.

"Where are you going?" Hazel asked. "I thought our business was in the barn."

Jaime kept pounding up the rickety steps. "Up here," she said, opening a small door at the top and stepping inside. "The animals are Maura and Craig's department. I don't do livestock, even if it *is* a gentleman's farm."

Hazel looked back at the horses in their stalls, their wide eyes dark and unblinking. "A gentleman's farm?"

"No killing or food production of any kind. It's all very civilized," Jaime said, motioning for Hazel to follow her into a small office at the top of the stairs. "Which doesn't make it smell any better in here, but you get used to it."

Hazel glanced around the office. It was a dark room, just big enough for a desk, a chair, and rows of beige-colored filing cabinets. Across the room was a second door and Hazel peered though it, down a long, narrow hallway.

"That's where the barn crew shacks up in the summer," Jaime explained. "There's always room, if you're interested."

Hazel's nose wrinkled and she shook her head, feeling lucky that she'd been assigned to the guesthouse. Even if it did mean more quality time with Jaime.

"Take a seat," Jaime commanded, standing with her arms crossed in front of the cabinets. Hazel sunk into the tall rolling chair.

Jaime reached forward and tugged out one of the top drawers. Inside, color-coded folders were arranged and labeled alphabetically. "Billy broke the treadmill again," Jaime said, quickly flipping through the files. "I know the manual is in here somewhere, but I haven't had a chance to find it."

Jaime reached both hands into the cabinet and lugged out a fat folder, overflowing with yellowing manuals for what looked like every single electronic device the Scotts had ever purchased. She dropped the folder in Hazel's lap, sending the chair rolling backward until Hazel was wedged between the desk and the wall.

"Have fun, Blondie," Jaime cooed as she wiped the dust from her hands and started back down the stairs.

"It's Hazel," Hazel shot back, slapping the file onto the desk.

Jaime popped her head back around the corner, dark ringlets bouncing around her forehead. "What was that?"

"My name isn't Blondie, it's Hazel," Hazel repeated. "And I'm sorry you don't want me here, but Rosanna does. I have no idea what your problem is."

"Problem? I don't have a problem," Jaime said flatly. "And even if I did have a problem—which I don't—I can't imagine you'd understand. I heard all about your parents and their little European vacation. Sounds swell." Jaime's voice dripped with false sincerity.

Hazel's pulse raged in her ears and she wanted nothing more than to set the record straight, to snap back with her real story, the one without vacations or parents of any kind.

"You sure it's too late to join them?" Jaime asked with a dramatic pout.

Hazel's cheeks were burning and she turned quickly back to the folder on the desk.

"Later, Blondie," Jaime called as she bounded down the stairs. Through the office's one, blurry window, Hazel watched as Jaime stalked across the field. The tall, leafy oaks swayed in the breeze and there wasn't a cloud in the sky. In the distance, the ocean looked striped, the sun reflected in mirrored streaks across the surface.

Hazel sighed and opened the folder.

A beautiful day for paperwork.

10

*H*azel's eyes were swimming and her head throbbed. After she'd come back for the treadmill manual, Jaime had quickly assigned Hazel an endless list of boring tasks, ranging from sorting the unpaid bills to testing an entire box full of printer cartridges.

Hazel was also starving. Jaime had brought her a dry turkey sandwich at lunch, but that was hours ago. She had no idea how late she was supposed to stay in the office and was considering making a run for it, when a pair of voices wafted from behind the door to the hall. She hopped out of the chair and peeked through the window, like a prisoner in solitary confinement, ravenous as much for conversation as she was for a decent meal.

A muscular girl with braided blond pigtails walked toward her, followed by a lanky boy with a dark goatee. They both looked to be in their mid-twenties. They stopped at a door and were about to disappear behind it when Hazel burst into the hall.

"Hi!" she said, with just a touch more enthusiasm than

she'd hoped. "I mean, hey. I'm Hazel. I'm . . . working here now. With Jaime?"

The girl took a step toward her and wiped her hands on the sides of her dirty overalls. "Oh, hey. Rosanna told us to be on the lookout for a new face." She smiled. Her face was dotted with freckles. "I'm Maura, and this is Craig." Craig offered an awkward little wave and ducked inside one of the rooms off of the hall.

"Sorry, were we bothering you?" Maura asked, peering over Hazel's shoulder into the office. "Feeding time can get pretty chaotic."

"Not at all," Hazel insisted. "I was just starting to go a little stir crazy."

Maura laughed, her braids swinging behind her back. "We're about to head down to the beach for the bonfire," she explained. "It's sort of a weekly tradition. You should come."

At home, Hazel was well practiced in the art of turning down invitations, and rarely saw anybody outside of school or work. But suddenly she found herself feeling grateful for even the possibility of being around people. Especially people other than Jaime. She smiled. "Thanks. I'd like that."

"Cool." Maura nodded, heading back toward her door. "Let me clean up and we'll meet you downstairs?"

Hazel nodded and closed herself back inside the tiny office. Jaime would probably be mad she hadn't gotten to everything, and even more annoyed when Hazel showed up at the bonfire. But Hazel didn't care.

In fact, it only made her want to go more.

The sun was low in the sky as Craig led the girls down a long, wooded path. Mosquitoes buzzed around their heads and Hazel swatted at one as it nibbled near her ankle. The path ended at a clearing in the forest, where ten or twelve cars, mostly pickup trucks and beat-up hatchbacks, were already parked. They took a rickety old staircase to the beach and Hazel reminded herself not to look down.

On the beach, Maura and Craig kicked their shoes into a pile by the dunes. Hazel did the same, letting her toes sink into the cool, damp sand. The wood was collected in a hole dug up at the edge of the cliffs, and Hazel watched as a group of scruffy-faced older guys arranged it in a pyramid, attempting to light the bottom with a match.

"There're burgers and hot dogs," Craig said, pointing across the fire to where Emmett was arranging patties on a charcoal grill.

"Veggie, too, if you want," Maura added, bending down to roll up the cuffs of her jeans.

"Thanks," Hazel said, glancing quickly at the crowd as she followed Craig over to a blue plastic cooler. "Are Rosanna and Billy coming?"

"Doubt it." Craig shrugged as he grabbed a handful of beers from the cooler and offered them around. Hazel politely declined, as Maura tapped the top of her can twice with dirt-caked fingernails before popping it open.

"They let us do our own thing at night," Maura explained. "Rosanna rocks."

Hazel felt a mix of disappointment and secret pride. She wanted to know more. If she couldn't spend time with Rosanna, she at least wanted to be learning as much as she could.

"Heads up," a familiar voice called from the shore.

Hazel looked out toward the water. Standing just a few yards away was Prince Charming himself, the chestnut-haired guy from the ice-cream shop. Before she could say anything he tossed her a can of beer, lobbing it through the air in a high, impressive arc. She caught it with two hands, the cold aluminum biting her palms.

"Hey, Luke," Maura called as he joined them. His hair was shaggier and longer than Hazel remembered, and even in the dark there was a glimmer in his deep brown eyes.

"That's creative," Craig joked as the boys slapped five. "Throwing things at the new girl. Kind of like kindergarten all over again."

Luke laughed. He was wearing baggy cargo shorts that came to his knees and a hunter green T-shirt. One sleeve was pushed up higher than the other and she could see the line where his tan ended beneath it. She was surprised at how relieved she felt to be seeing him again—as if she'd been waiting for him to show up.

"Oh, we go way back," Luke insisted, nudging Hazel with his elbow. "Guess those directions I gave you worked out."

"Looks that way." Hazel nodded, and held her arms closer to her sides. Maura and Craig set off for a walk on the beach, and Hazel looked down at the sand, tracing a line with her toe.

"So . . . ," Luke began. "How's it going so far?"

He settled down into the sand and patted the space beside him. Hazel lowered herself carefully to the ground, tucking her bare feet beneath her legs. She wished she'd had the sense to grab a sweater. The sun had almost slipped completely below the water line and the air was already crisp and cool.

"Okay." She shrugged. "I got the job."

"I had a feeling you would," Luke said, taking a long sip of his beer. Hazel looked down at the can in her hands and tapped it with her fingers, as she'd seen Maura do. She'd only been to a few official parties in her life, one or two with her college-aged coworkers at the pharmacy. But she knocked back a full swig, trying not to make a face. The beer was bitter and not as cold as the can let on.

"How do you know Maura and Craig?" Hazel asked, swallowing hard. She wedged her can in the sand and twisted it in tight little circles.

"It's a small island," Luke said, before turning to face her with a sly grin. "And it's an even smaller barn."

Hazel looked up sharply as he leaned back and dug his elbows into the sand. "You live in the barn?"

"I do." Luke nodded and stretched his long legs. His shins were tanned and strong-looking, with a layer of dark blond hair. "I looked for you yesterday, but I figured you had your hands full with Jaime."

As if on cue, Jaime shuffled past them, looking at the growing fire. She wore an oversize sweatshirt and cutoff shorts, and Hazel noticed for the first time that her knees were slightly turned in, just like her own. Not like they'd ever bond over that, or anything.

Luke whistled through his teeth, raising his can as Jaime turned. Jaime started to wave back, but quickly stuffed her hand in her pocket as soon as she spotted Hazel.

"I'm guessing I was right," Luke hedged.

Hazel sighed and took another sip from the can. This one went down somewhat easier. She could already feel a lightness spreading across her chest.

"Do you work on the farm, too?" Hazel asked. She was still trying to wrap her head around the fact that he slept only a few feet away from where she'd been holed up in the office all day. She hated being oblivious to things that were right in front of her. It made her feel like there was a secret code, and everyone knew it but her.

"Nah." Luke shook his head, wiping sand from the heels of his palms. "I work at the yacht club in town. But I've been staying at Rosanna's every summer since I was a little kid."

Hazel felt a quick jealous pang. Had everyone at the estate been living with Rosanna and Billy forever? She imagined a younger Luke, playing in the waves, feeding the animals, eating family dinners at the patio table. They were *her* parents, but it seemed like Luke and the others already had something with them that she never would.

"What about your parents?" Hazel asked. The question came out with more of an edge than she'd meant for it to. "I mean, where do you live the rest of the year?"

"I was born in Virginia, but we moved around a lot," Luke explained. "My dad's a military defense lawyer. I made it to about the sixth grade before he had me shipped off to boarding school. Guess I should be grateful. After living with him, school was a walk in the park."

"Where did you go?" Hazel asked. She'd always wondered what it would be like to go to boarding school. It sounded kind of nice, actually. During the school year, nobody had parents. Maybe she would've actually fit in.

"A couple places." Luke shrugged. "Mostly in Maryland and D.C. Took a while to find the right spot. But I survived."

Hazel stared at a patch of sand by her feet. She'd always

thought that knowing who her parents were would automatically mean she'd get to live in one place forever.

"What about you?" Luke asked. "I heard you're from California. How'd you end up out here?"

Hazel tucked her hands inside the long sleeves of her shirt and let her hair fall over her shoulder, hoping it would effectively shield her face. She'd told the lie a few times now, but it still felt awkward on her tongue.

"My parents are traveling," she said loudly, in that voice she sometimes used when she was called on in class and hadn't been paying attention. It was a kind of fake confidence that she hoped would hide the fact that she had no idea what she was saying. "I didn't have anything else to do."

At least that part was true, and Luke seemed to buy the rest. "What about when the summer ends?" he asked. "Back to school?"

Hazel looked out at the water, and thought of the sterile halls of her high school, the anonymous cafeteria where she ate alone at lunch. The night of the party at the Ferry Building, she'd had only a few months until graduation. She hadn't given much thought to what came next. There was that art school in the city, but she still didn't think it was worth the tuition. And she couldn't imagine ever living in New York.

"I have no idea," she sighed, and Luke laughed. A Frisbee skidded to a stop beside them and Luke grabbed for it. He looked toward the water and tossed it to a stocky kid with a crew cut, waving one hand over his head.

"Join the club," Luke said, clapping sand from between his fingers. "I always thought I'd have a better idea of what I wanted by now. I'm not all that worried about it, but my mom is convinced I'm throwing my life away by not going to college."

"Were you planning on it?" Hazel asked.

"I guess. I mean, I'm definitely not enlisting, which is what my dad thinks I should do," he said. "I don't know. I talked to Rosanna about it. She's the only one who understands anything."

Hazel hugged her knees to her chest and rested her chin on her forearms. "She seems really great," she said, the same mix of pride and confusion battling inside of her. She loved hearing people saying nice things about her mother. But a familiar knot was twisting in her stomach. If all of the amazing things she'd heard were true, if Rosanna was so understanding and generous and kind, why had she given Hazel up at all? Now that she was seeing all that she'd been missing out on first-hand, it was hard not to feel even more disappointed.

Luke buried his heels deeper in the sand. "She's the best," he said plainly. "I have no idea what would happen to me if I didn't have this place to come back to every year."

Hazel turned to look at Luke, his profile glowing in the burnt orange light of the flames behind him. She had never talked this way with anyone, let alone a boy. The idea that he was actually, in the real world, more than twice her age, flitted across her conscience for a moment. But talking to him was so easy and comfortable that it was hard to remember it wasn't real.

Luke turned back from the water, the whites of his eyes glistening as he held her gaze. Hazel wanted to look away but couldn't.

"I'm glad you saw that sign in town." He smiled, his brown eyes warm and inviting. "I knew Aunt Ro would love that dress." His hand moved closer to hers and he nudged her teasingly with one bent elbow.

Hazel squirmed from his touch, bolting upright. "Aunt Ro?" she repeated.

Luke was still leaning toward her, his fingers brushing against hers.

"Rosanna," he said quietly. "She's my mom's sister. I just had a feeling you two would—"

Hazel sprung to her feet in one quick motion, nearly trampling Luke's hand. Without a word, she turned and scurried back toward the steps.

"What happened?" Luke called after her, pushing himself up to standing as she started to climb to the top. "Where are you going?"

"I have to go back," she called over her shoulder, every thud of her heartbeat exploding in her ears. "I'm sorry. I have to go."

She could feel Luke on her heels and hurried to put more distance between them. Rosanna was his aunt. He was her *cousin*. Hazel felt sick.

"Do you want me to walk you?" Luke asked. Hazel glanced back at him again. His wide eyes were puzzled and searching. "It's dark."

Hazel paused, her hand on the splintered railing. "No," she said. Her mind spun in dizzying circles. "I need to be alone."

Luke stood frozen, looking up at her for a long moment before stuffing his hands in his pockets and slouching back to the bottom step. He kicked at the sand before turning and walking back toward the fire.

Hazel watched him go, her breathing shallow and hard. She started back up the stairs, the dim light of the moon her only guide as she struggled to find her way.

11

The next morning, Hazel followed Jaime toward the barn, yawning and dragging her feet across the lawn. She hadn't gotten much sleep. Every time she closed her eyes she saw the hurt look on Luke's face when she'd left him by the fire. And then the dizzy sick feeling was back, lurking inside her belly. In the light of day, it was almost funny. Of course the first guy she'd ever cared about getting to know would be her biological relative. Of course.

"Rosanna wants your help today," Jaime said, stopping abruptly in front of the studio and swatting the screen door open. Hazel looked up quickly, unable to stop the smile that was stretching across her lips. She couldn't tell what she was happier about: the prospect of spending time with Rosanna, or the idea of an entire day without Jaime.

"She needs you to price some pieces for the show," Jaime added, leaning over a low, mahogany table by the door and shuffling through a tall pile of papers.

"The show?" Hazel repeated, as Jaime lifted a heavy black binder and plopped it into her hands.

"Tomorrow night," Jaime said, already halfway back out the door. "Rosanna's having an art show in town. Last year tons of people came, though I'm pretty sure it was mostly for the free food."

Hazel nodded and opened up the binder. Pages and pages of spreadsheets and numbers were separated by colored folders and tabs. She felt her smile fading as the tiny print blurred in her vision. More paperwork. How fun.

"There are stickers in the pocket," Jaime directed. "Match the numbers on the price list with the ones on the back of the canvases. It's not rocket science."

Jaime swung through the screen door and started off toward the woods. Hazel watched until the girl had disappeared before dropping the binder heavily back onto the table. It was her first time alone in the studio and she wasn't going to waste it staring at spreadsheets. At least, not yet.

Hazel crouched on her knees by the table and flipped through a pile of Rosanna's paintings, some finished and framed, and some on stretched canvases waiting to be mounted. There were landscapes, many featuring the farm and nearby ponds, as well as intimate portraits. But even the paintings wider in scope seemed to focus somehow on a person, a face.

Hazel held out a smallish portrait of an older man fishing off a dock. The lines in his face were deep, and they faded into the shadow of the horizon behind his head. Hazel couldn't believe how much expression Rosanna had captured in his dark, thoughtful eyes.

For the first time since she'd woken up on the boat, Hazel thought of her camera. She never took pictures of people, ever. It wasn't like she'd spent a lot of time thinking about that fact; the opportunity just never came up. Who would she ask? She certainly wasn't going to go up to a stranger on the street. And she never thought about photography as having anything to do with the people in the pictures. She took pictures because it was the only way she knew she existed. *I was here.* It was about anchoring herself in a moment, when everything else seemed to be floating off in the distance. It was a strange, personal connection, and she couldn't imagine anybody else ever being involved.

But as her eyes examined the fisherman's leathery face, Hazel couldn't help but feel inspired. The portraits were so powerful. Maybe she should try branching out.

Hazel leaned the fisherman back up against the wall and stood, her foot accidentally knocking a framed canvas onto its side. She lifted it up, and gasped when she realized it was a painting of Luke. He was crouching over the front end of a small sailboat, hooking a rope around a metal cleat, his jaw set in concentration. Even from the side, Rosanna had managed to highlight his dimples and the mischievous gleam in his eyes.

Hazel quickly flipped the frame facedown and grabbed the binder off of the table. It was time to get to work. She didn't want to be bothering with things like stickers and price lists when Rosanna came back.

Two hours later, when all of the paintings had been priced and Rosanna was still nowhere to be found, Hazel grew tired of waiting. Jaime hadn't told her what to do next, and Hazel was sick of spending so much time alone. She hadn't needed a dressmaking fairy godmother—or to go back in time and across the country, for that matter—to do any more of that.

Hazel left the binder on the table and made her way across the lawn to the main house. She slid open the glass door to the kitchen, secretly hoping to find Emmett armed with more breakfast treats. But the house was quiet. The only sound was the gentle swirling of a ceiling fan and the echo of surf on the rocks.

Hazel was about to give up when she heard the murmur of voices at the other end of the front hall. She tiptoed past a long wall of photos. There were a few of Rosanna and Billy, many of Billy and Buster the dog, and one of Luke with a woman who could've been Rosanna's twin—clearly Luke's mom. *My aunt*, Hazel thought with a shiver of disbelief. There was even a photo of Jaime, looking young and happy and sitting atop a carousel horse.

The hallway wrapped around another wing of the house, and as Hazel followed, stepping carefully on the polished floorboards, the voices grew louder and more intense. One voice was much louder and angrier than the rest, and Hazel realized that they were coming from a door at the end of the hall. She saw a flickering shadow beneath the door and turned quickly on her heels, but it was too late.

The door swung open and Jaime stormed out, her cheeks flushed and her dark eyes red and raw. Hazel stepped to one side, ready with an excuse of needing a bathroom break. But Jaime silenced her with a look as she passed.

Seconds later, Luke appeared in the hall, his eyebrows drawn and his mouth pursed and serious. "Jaime," he called after her. But she was already at the front door. "Jaime, wait!"

"Leave me alone!" Hazel heard her call through an open window in the foyer. She could feel Luke breathing at her shoulder, and they watched together as Jaime disappeared into the woods.

"She'll be all right," a fragile voice spoke behind them and Hazel turned around. Rosanna stood at the open door. She looked as put-together as ever in a cable-knit white cardigan and dark jeans, but her eyes looked tired, her skin tighter and drained.

The room behind her was one that Hazel hadn't seen before, and from the hulking computers and dark leather furniture she guessed it was Billy's office.

Rosanna put a hand on Luke's shoulder and squeezed. "Just give her some time," she said. Her eyes quickly landed on Hazel and she paused, as if considering whether or not she should say any more, and then stepped back into the office. The door snapped shut behind her.

Hazel stood glued to the floorboards. Her blood was pounding in her temples, and she didn't know what to say.

Luke shoved his hands in his pockets and stared at the office door. His shoulders were slumped and he looked somehow smaller than he had the night before.

"Are you okay?" Hazel asked. She felt like she needed to say something. After the way she'd run out on him at the bonfire, she at least owed him that.

Luke looked up at her, as if he'd forgotten she was there. "Yeah," he said, forcing a smile. "I think I just need some air."

Hazel nodded and watched as he started down the hall.

"Coming?" he asked from the front door.

Surprised by the invitation, Hazel hurried to meet him on the porch.

They walked along the path to the beach, past the wooden staircase at the cliff, and onto a trail in the woods. The trail led to a clearing and a small pond that Hazel recognized from one of Rosanna's paintings.

Hazel stole sideways glances at Luke as they walked. His head was down and he seemed to be seeing nothing but the tops of his green striped flip-flops.

"Sorry," he said eventually, stopping at a crooked wooden dock that jutted out into the water. "Sometimes I just need to walk."

Hazel stopped beside him and followed his gaze down the dock. The pond was still and dotted with lily pads. It looked like something out of a picture book.

"It's okay," she said. "It's none of my business. You don't have to say anything if you don't want to."

Luke shook his head and looked up at her. His light eyes looked cloudy and sad.

"You're going to find out eventually," he said. "And you're a part of things here now. It *is* your business."

Luke held her stare for a moment before shuffling out to the end of the dock. Hazel walked after him, her head spinning. She'd never really been a part of anything before. Even if it was bad news, she couldn't help but feel the tiniest twinge of hope at the idea that she was about to be included.

At the end of the dock, they sat, their feet dangling over the water. The reflection of a tall row of evergreens rippled across the pond's surface, and dragonflies zipped between their ankles. Luke fiddled with a stick he'd found, snapping off little nubs with his fingers.

"Rosanna's sick," he said. "She has cancer."

Hazel's heart dropped, and her palms were suddenly cold. She closed her eyes, her mind flashing back to the night before she'd left California. The conversation she'd overheard between the couple at the buffet.

"It all happened so fast."

"Rosanna was so strong."

Rosanna's death had seemed sudden. A surprise. Hazel had never considered the possibility that she'd have already been sick, eighteen years in the past.

"Are you . . ." Hazel's mind raced, and she didn't know what she was trying to ask. "Are you sure?"

Luke nodded. "We've all known for a while," he explained. "But now it's getting worse. She needs more treatment, but the doctors aren't sure if it will work."

Hazel stared beyond Luke at the trees, his profile blurring into a neutral smudge. Suddenly, a wave of relief passed through her, softening the strong line of her brow, loosening the muscles she hadn't realized she was holding tight.

It will *work,* she thought. The doctors were wrong. Rosanna wasn't getting worse, at least not for a while. She had eighteen years ahead of her. And when the alternative was tomorrow, eighteen years seemed like a very long time.

Hazel looked quickly back to Luke, her eyes wide and hopeful.

But there was absolutely nothing she could say. There was no way to explain how she knew the things she knew. Not without sounding insane.

"I'm sorry," she finally managed. She *was* sorry. Sorry she couldn't do anything to make him understand that it wasn't as bad as any of them feared.

"There's more," Luke said quietly. "They're selling the estate. Rosanna is going to need to be in San Francisco full-time, until her treatments are over. And afterward, it will be too much for them to keep coming back and forth. My mom was even surprised that Rosanna wanted to make the trip this year," he mused, looking out at the water. "I guess they wanted the chance to say good-bye."

Hazel gripped the edge of the dock with her fingers. She wanted so badly to tell Luke that he wouldn't have to say good-bye. Not yet. She even wanted to run and find Jaime to tell her the good news, too.

"Jaime's taking it the hardest, I think," Luke said, as if reading her mind. "She's the only one of us who lives here all year long. And she and Rosanna have always been close."

Hazel nodded. She remembered the way she'd felt when she ran out of the Ferry Building and cried on the boat. She'd thought there could be nothing worse than losing somebody before you'd even gotten the chance to know her. Now she wondered if she'd been wrong. Maybe knowing was worse.

Luke shifted by her side, leaning forward to toss the twig into the pond. "Anyway," he said. "I just thought you should know. It's actually probably why she hired you in the first place. Rosanna and Jaime will both need a lot of help getting everything ready. It's not going to be easy."

His voice was soft but there was distance inside of it. He sounded like he was talking to a coworker. Hazel looked up at him. The glimmer in his eyes was still there, but it looked stifled and far away. He was uncomfortable talking to her, and Hazel knew why.

"Luke," she said, turning to him. "I'm sorry about last night."

Instantly, he blushed, pink patches spreading beneath the surface of his smooth, tanned skin. His eyes darted back to the pond. "Don't worry about it," he muttered. "I understand."

Hazel laughed choppily before she could stop herself. "No," she said. "You don't. But that's okay. I just want you to know that it's not what you think. You're . . . great. You're all great. And of course I'll help. I'll do everything I can. All right?"

He glanced back at her, confusion knitting his brow. "Sure," he said tentatively. "All right. Thanks."

Hazel turned back out to the pond, biting the inside of her lip, her feet swinging above the water's edge.

"I should get to work," Luke said, crawling to his feet. "See you around?"

Hazel peered up at him and smiled. "I'll be here," she said.

Luke opened his hand in a little wave and started back toward the shore.

"Luke?" Hazel called after him from the dock.

He turned. "Yeah?"

Hazel swallowed and tugged at a stray piece of hair clinging to the side of her cheek. "It's going to be okay," she said. "Okay?"

Luke nodded and waved again, before disappearing behind the trees.

Hazel looked back at the water. She swung her feet harder now, and felt her bare heels skip along the cool, wet surface.

Now, it all made sense. Rosanna already knew she was sick. She thought she didn't have much time left. That's why she'd given Hazel up. She hadn't wanted Hazel to grow up without a mother, and so she did what she had to do. She found her a new one. It was the only possible explanation. Why else would somebody so wonderful, and so obviously ready to be a mother, not want to raise her own daughter herself?

Hazel hopped to her feet. For the first time since she'd woken up on the boat, she finally felt like she knew what she was sent back to the island to do.

But first, she'd need another dress.

12

The sun was in no hurry to set.

Hazel was perched at the edge of her bed, her knees bouncing up and down. After dinner— Emmett's crab cakes and a summer salad, eaten on the patio— Hazel had rushed back to the guesthouse and flung open the closet door. Jaime had disappeared before dessert, and Hazel was relieved. She had no idea what kind of lame excuse she'd rattle off if Jaime caught her, sitting alone, staring out the window, and wearing a gown.

Because that's exactly what the dress was: a gown. Made of rose-colored silk, it had subtle accents: a muted trail of flowers at the hem, and a delicate chain that dangled from the clasp. Hazel had stopped breathing when she'd pulled it out of the bag. It was, hands down, the most beautiful thing she'd ever seen.

But it would be a nightmare to explain.

Which was why she had waited until dark. Once the sun finally tucked itself behind the glowing horizon, a shadow falling over the fields, Hazel ran barefoot out of the cabin and down to the path in the woods.

She'd known right away that the pond was where she was headed. It was the perfect place to make her second wish. It was there that she'd had the idea, after all, and something about the stillness of the water, and the cover of the towering trees, already felt like magic.

Hazel followed the path to the dock where she'd sat with Luke. The moon was full and white in the indigo sky. She closed her eyes, a soft breeze rustling the cool silk against her legs.

She was ready to make her wish. All afternoon she'd been thinking of the exact words, the perfect turn of phrase. If Rosanna only knew. If she knew she had eighteen full years ahead of her, she wouldn't be so scared. And when she discovered that she was having a baby—which, if it hadn't happened already, would have to happen soon—she wouldn't give her up. Of course she'd want to keep her. Hazel knew she would.

And everything would be different. Hazel would grow up with her real parents. She'd be loved and cared for, not shuffled around like a piece of lost luggage. She'd grow up with answers instead of questions. With an idea of the kind of person she was supposed to be. It was exactly what she'd always wanted, and this was her chance to make it real.

Hazel had spent the day rereading Posey's letter in her mind. Curing Rosanna wasn't an option; it was too big, too "universal." But what about wishing for Rosanna to make a different choice? Wishing for Rosanna to keep her, and raise her, for as long as she could?

Hazel took a deep breath. She saw the words, lit up like

fireflies inside of her. She was about to whisper them out loud, when she heard a faint whimpering coming from behind her on the shore.

It sounded like a bird at first. Hazel opened her eyes and turned, waiting for another sound. But all was quiet.

Hazel turned back to the water and closed her eyes again. As soon as she'd taken a full, steadying breath, the distant whimper was back, this time followed by a rustling of leaves.

Hazel lifted up the edge of her dress and walked back toward the shore, the old dock creaking beneath her feet.

The noises grew louder, and Hazel followed them along the edge of the marsh. Just beyond a cluster of beech trees was a rusted metal bench. A figure was huddled in one corner, and she could tell from the silhouette of dark, springy curls that it was Jaime.

Hazel stopped short. Jaime hadn't seen her yet. There was still time to turn around. Jaime would probably want to be left alone, anyway. She'd been upset and keeping to herself all day. Maybe Hazel could sneak back to the guesthouse without Jaime ever knowing she was there.

But it was as if her feet refused to move in any direction other than toward the shadowed bench. And her heart knew why. She had done her fair share of crying to herself, and never once had she been grateful to go through it alone. Even a misguided something was always better than nothing at all.

"Jaime?" Hazel started quietly, hovering at the far end of the wrought-iron bench. It wasn't the most comfortable-looking piece of furniture, and Hazel marveled at how small Jaime had managed to make herself, perched between the wide metal bars. "Are you okay?"

Jaime's head was buried in the sleeve of her hooded sweatshirt and she didn't move to answer. "Do I look okay?"

Hazel glanced back at the pond, the pitched roof of the cabin looming on the other side. She could have made her wish and been back to her room by now. If only she'd just kept walking.

"Do you want me to get someone?" Hazel asked. Maybe if she could pass Jaime off to somebody else, somebody Jaime would actually talk to, they could all pretend like this never happened. "Rosanna, maybe?"

Jaime snorted, her shoulders heaving in a sarcastic chuckle, which gradually stretched into longer, quieter sobs. Hazel looked away. There was something about seeing someone as tough as Jaime cry that felt wrong, like it almost shouldn't be possible. It was the first time Jaime had let her guard down, even if it was accidental, and Hazel knew she was in too deep to just walk away now.

She slowly lowered herself to the bench beside Jaime. While she knew that some people were the "just sit with me while I cry" type, she had a strong feeling that Jaime was not one of these people. She was going to have to say something.

"Luke told me about Rosanna," Hazel began, her voice low and soft. So soft, in fact, that when Jaime didn't say anything back right away, Hazel wondered if she hadn't heard her. "I'm sorry," she said, her voice cracking and loud.

Jaime turned away, her breathing shaky and shallow. Hazel squeezed her knees together and tried again. "You've been living here for a while, right?" she asked. "It must be hard to think about leaving."

"I don't care about leaving," Jaime spat, sniffing and

slapping at the wet corners of her eyes. "I don't care about anything, okay?"

Hazel's pulse throbbed in her veins. Something in Jaime's voice sounded so familiar. Cold, lost, and aloof. It was the voice she'd heard deep inside herself, on all of the nights she'd been alone. Convincing herself that nothing mattered. Nobody else cared. Why should she?

"Jaime," Hazel started again, gripping the bench's cool railing. "I know it's scary, Rosanna being sick. And I know how much she means to you, but—"

"You don't know anything," Jaime blurted, and turned her face toward the woods, her shoulders rocking against the tops of her folded knees.

Hazel sat quietly beside her. Jaime was wrong; Hazel knew lots of things. But there wasn't anything she could say, and her vague sympathies were clearly only making the situation worse. Hazel sighed, ready to walk away, but something nagged at her to try one last time.

"Look, I know you don't like me very much. But if you ever feel like you want to talk about it . . ."

"I don't!" Jaime shot at her, lifting her head and turning to face her with wild, bloodshot eyes. "I don't want to talk about it. And I don't even *know* you! How could I possibly like you? Just leave me alone!"

Hazel's face burned and she rose to her feet. She could think of a thousand things she'd rather have been doing than trying to comfort Jaime in the dark. And now she was being yelled at? For trying to be nice?

Hazel shook her head and started toward the dock. She was at the water's edge when she heard Jaime's voice. Her head was still pressed against her sleeve so the words were muffled and quiet. Hazel stopped and turned around. "Did you say something?" she asked quietly, half-hoping she'd imagined it.

Jaime raised her head and looked at her again. Her eyes were wide and empty, and her shoulders rose as she took a deep, calming breath. "If you tell anyone, I will kill you," she said. "I'm not kidding. I know where you sleep."

Hazel nodded. She felt the skin around her eyebrows tightening, her eyes burning from not blinking for so long. "Okay," she finally said. "What is it?"

Jaime looked past Hazel toward the water. Her eyes caught the reflection of the moon shining back from the pond, and her skin looked soft and smooth. In the quiet, and in this light, there was no doubt about it. Jaime was beautiful.

She took another deep breath and looked back to Hazel.

"I'm not upset because I have to move. I'm not even upset about Rosanna. I'm not *upset*," she insisted. "I'm pregnant."

13

"Wait here," Jaime said the next morning. "If I don't eat something, I'm going to hurl."

Hazel stood in front of a shingled shack at the harbor, watching numbly as cars poured off of the boat, returning to the mainland. She had agreed the night before to go with Jaime to the clinic, without realizing that it would involve taking a day off from work, taking the shuttle to town, getting back on the boat, and waiting at a bus stop for the better part of the morning.

Jaime returned with a candy bar from the vending machine and plopped onto the wooden bench. "I can't believe I let you talk me into this."

Hazel rolled her eyes. "You can't just take one over-the-counter test," she said. Not that she had any idea, but based on a few TV movies and one incredibly uncomfortable semester of Health and the Human Body, it seemed like going for a checkup was an important next step. "And if you're too scared to go to a clinic on the island . . ."

"I told you, I'm not *scared*," Jaime hissed. "I just don't want to deal with it. The secretary was my fourth-grade teacher. The nurse is Maura's stepmom."

Hazel kicked at the dusty ground. It was a spectacularly sunny day, and the water sparkled. It seemed almost surreal that she had agreed to make the trip with Jaime. But it wasn't as if she could really say no. If there had been anyone else for Jaime to ask, she would have. Hazel didn't flatter herself to think that she'd been Jaime's top choice.

The shuttle finally slowed to a stop in front of them, and Jaime took a seat up front, huddling herself against the window. Hazel watched as Jaime took out a beat-up-looking Discman—Hazel could hardly remember a time before iPods—and settled the bulky black headphones over her ears. Hazel found an empty seat across the aisle.

Part of Hazel felt relieved that they wouldn't have to talk, but another part of her was full of questions. How had this happened? Who was the father? Was it the boyfriend Emmett had mentioned? Why hadn't Hazel ever seen him around?

Hazel looked out the window, leaning in her seat as the shuttle took a sharp corner out of the parking lot. What was she *doing* here? She was hardly qualified to offer any kind of advice, not that Jaime would ever ask for it. Hazel had kissed only one boy in her life: Max, a neighbor in San Francisco who used to invite her over to play video games when his parents were at work. It had only happened once, and hardly lasted more than a second. She'd avoided him afterward, taking the long way around her block any time she needed to pass his building, and that was that.

It didn't make sense. She was just starting to get used to

the idea that she'd woken up in the past, across the country, and had been given a chance to get to know her mother while she was alive. And now here she was, taking day trips with Jaime, the one person she'd been trying to get away from since she'd gotten to the island.

It wasn't that she didn't feel bad for Jaime. She did. She couldn't imagine what must be going through Jaime's mind. Rosanna was sick, they were selling the estate, and now this? But, for the most part, the whole excursion seemed like a colossal waste of time.

The shuttle squealed to a stop and Hazel followed Jaime down to the curb.

Falmouth Center was a quaint little village, with souvenir shops and cafés similar to the ones on the Vineyard. But even though Hazel had spent only a few days on the island, she could already feel a mainland difference. It was a pace thing, maybe. Or just the buried knowledge that where she stood now was connected to the rest of the country, as opposed to the island, where it sort of always felt like floating. She didn't know why, but she missed it already.

Jaime ducked between two lanes of traffic and Hazel scurried to keep up. Across the street was a small brick building, set back from the road with a little oval sign swinging out front. FALMOUTH FREE WOMEN'S CLINIC, it read. Hazel paused at the sign, considering it carefully. Something was wrong with the wording. Was the clinic only for free women? But *Free Falmouth* would have sounded like a command.

"What are you doing?" Jaime huffed from the top of the stairs. "Why don't you just put out an ad in the paper? Jaime Wells is knocked up!"

Hazel hurried to meet Jaime at the door. Jaime stood with her hand on the knob, staring at her dirty sneakers. She was in her work clothes, patched jean cutoffs, and a faded blue and red Coca-Cola T-shirt. She didn't look old enough to get into a PG-13 movie on her own, let alone have any reason to be visiting a women's clinic. Free or otherwise.

Hazel stepped in front of Jaime and opened the other door. "Ready?" she asked, trying her best to sound warm and nurturing.

Jaime rolled her eyes and pushed her way inside. "Move."

The clinic waiting room was loud and crowded, which hadn't been part of the plan. Young mothers (most not as young as Jaime, but definitely not card-carrying adults) pushed strollers and jiggled unhappy newborns on their laps. On a low couch in the corner, an extremely pregnant woman was sprawled out with a washcloth on her forehead. It basically could have been a Public Service Announcement for saving oneself for marriage.

Or eternity.

Jaime did a quick survey of the room and, after deciding that she didn't recognize anyone, made her way to the receptionist. A heavy woman with frizzy blond hair and too much mascara passed Jaime a form on a clipboard. "Fill this out and take a seat," she ordered between sips from a can of orange soda.

Hazel found them a pair of seats by the door. She sat quietly while Jaime studied the form, the end of her pen tapping furiously against the metal clip at the top. Seated diagonally across from them was a young couple around their age. The girl had straight black hair down to her waist, and the guy was gripping the armrests of his chair like they were the only things keeping him from bolting. They were trying desperately not to make eye contact with each other or anyone else. Hazel swallowed hard and looked at the dirty gray carpet. The couple looked like they had a story to tell, and Hazel was pretty sure she didn't want to hear it.

"I guess this is it," Jaime said suddenly. "I mean, after this I'll know for sure."

Hazel looked up at her, wracking her brain for supportive things to say.

"It's better to know than, um . . . not . . . know" was her tepid contribution.

Jaime turned to face her. She had dark, deep circles under her eyes and her hair flew up in curls around her temples. She looked terrified.

"Wow," she said drily. "I sure hope you're not considering a career in motivational speaking."

Hazel's stomach flipped but soon the corners of Jaime's mouth pulled up and she was laughing. It was a sound Hazel hadn't heard before, and maybe it was the shock of seeing Jaime smile, but before she knew what was happening, Hazel was laughing, too. Soon they had to cover their mouths to keep quiet. Hazel felt suddenly like she could finally take full breaths again. She hadn't realized how long it had been since she'd laughed, either.

"Okay," Jaime said, taking a deep breath and evenly letting it out. "Here goes nothing."

She laid the form on the armrest and pushed herself up off the chair. The clipboard dropped to the floor and Hazel bent down to grab it. As she passed the board to Jaime, something caught her eye and she held on a moment longer.

"What are you doing?" Jaime asked, pulling the clipboard harder.

But Hazel's grip was tight. She stared at the printed form and around her everything was suddenly quiet. The high-pitched squeals of uncomfortable babies, the hushed conversations, the bland elevator music piped in through the walls. All of it faded away, and Hazel could see only two words.

At the top of the form, where Jaime's name should have been, she'd written two words. Two words Hazel had seen before.

After NAME OF PATIENT, it read:

ROSANNA SCOTT.

The two words that had changed Hazel's life once before were about to change it all over again.

14

"**A**m I interrupting?"

Hazel was huddled behind a green Dumpster outside of the clinic when she heard Jaime's voice. She steadied herself with one hand on the brick wall, dragging her weighted limbs to standing.

Everything that had happened since she'd fumbled her way out of the clinic was a blur. She remembered watching Jaime's back as it disappeared down a long hallway, and the next thing she knew she was on her knees behind the Dumpster, dry heaving and seeing spots.

Her brain was screaming at her, broken thoughts battling for attention.

Rosanna is my mother.

Rosanna is not my mother.

Jaime is my mother.

It just wasn't possible. Jaime was too young. Jaime looked nothing like her.

Jaime was kind of a bitch.

But the one, indisputable fact about Jaime was that she was standing behind a low wall of trimmed hedges, her face bobbing between the branches as she peered at Hazel on the other side. "What are you *doing*?" she asked, her voice sharp and bewildered as Hazel walked slowly toward the narrow path.

"Nothing," Hazel mumbled, wiping her mouth with the sleeve of her thin cotton sweater. "I guess I felt a little sick from the boat."

Jaime crossed her arms, cutting the cartoon image of the Coke bottle on her T-shirt in half. She rolled her eyes and reached into her pocket.

"Well, it looks like I'll be in charge of the morning sickness from here on out," she said flatly, slapping a folded packet of papers into Hazel's palm. Jaime turned on her heels and started walking, leaving Hazel to unfold the papers. It was information about the clinic, checklists, appointments, and a list of reference books.

"What To Expect When You're Expecting."

Hazel's head went numb again and a sharp pain pierced her in the side.

"Let's go, Blondie," Jaime called from the middle of the street. "We have a boat to catch."

"Wait," Hazel said, just loud enough for Jaime to hear her. An older couple in a convertible screeched to a stop as Jaime hopped back to the sidewalk.

"What is the problem?" Jaime huffed.

Hazel stared at the paperwork in her hand before glancing up at Jaime's face with tired, searching eyes. "Rosanna," Hazel managed. "Why did you use Rosanna's name on the forms?"

Jaime crossed her arms again and shrugged as if it was no

big deal. "I don't know," she muttered. "I guess I just got nervous. And it's not like Rosanna's ever going to come here. She can't even have kids."

Jaime's eyes were darting impatiently across the sidewalk, and Hazel felt her heart sink even lower. "Can't have kids?" she asked. "Why . . . why not?"

Hazel's head was pounding. Jaime had to be wrong. Rosanna was her mother. She *had* to be.

Jaime rolled her eyes and threw up her hands. "I don't know the details, Hazel, I just know she can't get pregnant. Why else would she keep us all around so long? There's not *that* much work to be done." Jaime looked back to the bus stop. "Can we please go now?" she asked.

Hazel swallowed, nodding numbly, and followed Jaime across the street.

Neither Jaime nor Hazel said much on the ferry ride home. Jaime sunk into another indoor seat, immediately fumbling for her headphones, and Hazel went for a walk on the deck. There was no way she could sit still and stare at the girl who was suddenly, apparently, her mother. They hadn't even pulled out of the harbor yet and already it was starting to feel like the longest forty-five minutes of her life.

Hazel walked upstairs to the top deck. She found an empty chair in the front row of low plastic seats, where the wind was the strongest. She could hardly keep her eyes open against the billowing gusts of sea air, but she didn't care. At least it gave her something real to fight against.

She thought back to the crowded waiting room. Jaime had used Rosanna's name at the clinic. Which meant that all of her medical records from the clinic would be under that name.

Which meant that when the records were transferred to the hospital where she was born, Rosanna's name would be on her birth certificate, not Jaime's. Whether she liked it or not, Jaime was her mother.

And she didn't like it, not one little bit. She didn't know why, but the only thing she could identify happening inside of her, the only feeling she had a name for, was rage. She was furious.

First, with Jaime. For being so careless. Clearly Jaime had made a decision to sleep with somebody and not use protection. Or, at least, not use it well. Not that she'd had much experience, but Hazel couldn't imagine ever being so cavalier.

Mostly because she couldn't imagine anything worse than getting stuck, so young, with a baby. It seemed like all people did was change their minds and make mistakes. At school, she'd walk down the halls with her head down, secretly watching the couples of the moment, holding hands by the lockers, or sucking each other's faces off in dark corners behind the gym. And though she knew that there had to be a part of her, somewhere, that was jealous, usually she just felt better off. Because she was also there watching when, a few months or even weeks later, those same couples threw eye-darts at each other across the cafeteria, after things turned sour. And things always, *always* turned sour.

And then, when each half of the couple decided to do it all over again, she'd watched all that from the sidelines, too. Holding new hands, sucking new faces, and pretending like this time it was going to last.

What kind of a person would want to bring a baby into something like that? What was Jaime thinking? It didn't make sense.

Rosanna made sense. Rosanna was supposed to be her mother. They looked alike. They had similar interests. Not to mention the fact that Rosanna was married and stable and, well, old enough to be her mother.

The more Hazel thought about it, the more she realized that she wasn't just mad at Jaime. She was mad at Rosanna, too. Why *couldn't* Rosanna have gotten pregnant? Why *couldn't* Rosanna be her mother? She knew it wasn't fair, and it definitely wasn't Rosanna's fault, but she couldn't help it. It was the way she felt.

Hazel opened her eyes and walked to the railing. The curves of the island were just starting to come into view. She took a deep breath and went back inside. Jaime was asleep, her bony knees curled up beside her on the bench. The laces of one of her low-top sneakers were untied and hanging down near the linoleum floor.

Without thinking, Hazel reached for her camera. She'd thrown it into her bag yesterday, after being inspired by the portraits in Rosanna's studio.

Hazel held the camera up to her eye, framing Jaime's sleeping face in the lens. But, like a magnet, her eyes were drawn back to the one untied sneaker. There was something about the droopy laces that seemed so sad, and so young.

She squared the shot in the viewfinder and snapped the picture. Jaime didn't move. Hazel lowered the camera and sat in the booth. With that one click, something had softened inside of her. She couldn't blame Jaime for being scared. Maybe using Rosanna's name was her way of protecting herself. Of keeping herself separate from the situation, for as long as she could.

Hazel could imagine doing something like that.

Plus, it was hard to stay angry at somebody so scared and alone.

Especially when that somebody was about to become your mother.

15

*I*n all of the morning's activity, Hazel had completely forgotten about Rosanna's art show that evening. Jaime had an afternoon shift at the ice-cream shop, so Hazel caught the shuttle home alone, arriving just in time to help Luke and the others pack up the truck and head back into town.

The opening was held in an old hotel at the bottom of Main Street, and Hazel, Maura, and Craig spent most of the afternoon hanging paintings in the lobby and along the winding hallways of every floor. The idea was for guests to wander the halls on their way up to the rooftop lounge, which had been decorated with twinkling white lights and pink orchids nestled in every corner. Luke was in charge of the bar, while the rest of the crew served as on-call caterers.

It wasn't until Hazel and Jaime's third trip up in the service elevator that night, armed with trays of shrimp toasts and mini quiches, that either of them said anything about what had happened.

"How are you feeling?" Hazel finally managed to ask,

staring at her own reflection in the mirrored glass. Her auburn roots were thick at the top of her head, and her hair looked flat and strawlike from the sun.

"I don't know," Jaime mumbled. "Terrible. Disgusting. The same."

Hazel stared at the glowing metallic numbers as the elevator carried them up.

"Did you read any of that packet?" she asked. Jaime had threatened to throw the materials from the clinic overboard as they were getting off the boat, and Hazel made her swear to at least look through the whole thing once.

"Cover to cover," Jaime said, her voice slick and phony. "Did you know that my *baby* is already the size of a BB pellet?"

Hazel felt a lump growing in her throat, her knees turning to liquid. There was no way she could keep this up. BB pellet? That was *her* in there. How was she supposed to act like everything was normal, when she was living in some kind of sci-fi soap opera?

"Cool," Hazel forced, only it came out shaky and sounded kind of like she was choking.

"Totally," Jaime deadpanned as the elevator slammed into place. The doors started to click open, but Jaime jabbed at a button with her thumb, holding them shut.

"Listen," she said, suddenly serious as she looked Hazel in the eye. "Obviously, I'm not telling anybody about this until, you know, I've thought about it more. Which means you're not telling anybody, either. Got it?"

Hazel nodded quickly. "Of course," she said. "Got it."

"Good," Jaime sighed. For a moment, her dark eyes were soft, and Hazel could almost see her own reflection in them.

The doors shifted open, revealing the twilight sky in purple patches overhead. Hazel took a step outside but Jaime stopped her with a tight hand on the back of her elbow. "Wait," Jaime barked, tugging Hazel back inside. "One more thing."

Hazel turned, shifting the heavy tray from one open palm to the other. "What?" she whispered, glancing quickly from the crowd of guests on the roof back to Jaime.

Jaime took a deep breath and shook a few drooping curls out of her face.

"Just," she said, so quietly it was almost nothing at all, "thanks. For today. Okay?"

And then she was gone, brushing past Hazel and strutting deliberately through the groups of women in linen and men in summery suits.

Hazel followed Jaime through the crowd, stopping to offer snacks to anyone with a tiny paper plate. She felt her lips forming an automatic smile and did her best to make small talk. But it was impossible to think of anything else.

"You must love working for Rosanna," a guest would say, by way of conversation. And Hazel would nod, silently finishing the thought on her own.

I do. I used to think she was my mother.

"I just adore the portraits this year. Rosanna is so gifted, isn't she?"

Yes. She is. But she's not my mother.

The night slipped by in a fog. After Rosanna's welcome speech, Hazel sneaked over to the bar to ask Luke for a glass of water. He had his hands full mixing drinks and being generally charming. It seemed like every older woman in attendance had posted up in his section, fawning over his clean khaki jacket and striped silk tie, or tousling his shaggy brown hair.

Hazel helped herself to the pitcher of water, silently agreeing with Luke's admirers. He certainly cleaned up nice. The now-familiar sinking reminder that he was her cousin crept up inside of her . . . which was about when she realized that he wasn't.

He wasn't her cousin, because Rosanna wasn't her mother. She and Luke weren't related at all.

The revelation was so sharp and jarring that soon she was pouring water all over her wrist. She pulled the pitcher back and shook her hand dry behind the bar, hoping nobody had been watching.

"Thirsty?" Luke asked with a grin. He was reaching for a bottle of tonic water from the cooler when he caught Hazel in the act of cleaning up. "Try this," he said, tossing her the cloth napkin he had tucked in the back pocket of his pants.

Hazel snatched the napkin out of the air and patted her forearm dry. "Th-thanks," she stammered. She felt her cheeks reddening and hoped he wasn't still looking at her. Yesterday they were cousins, and today he was making her blush? It was all too weird for Hazel to handle. She chugged a few sips of water and hurried back into the crowd.

Hazel had just replenished the cheese plates when Rosanna stopped her in the second-floor hall. "What do you think?" she asked, reaching for a cracker and popping it into her mouth. "Is everyone having a good time?"

Hazel nodded and looked down at the carpeted hotel floor. "I hope so," she said. She hadn't quite gotten over the irrational anger she'd felt on the boat, and had been avoiding Rosanna all night. Every time she caught a glimpse of her on the roof, chatting with friends, she remembered the way she'd felt the first time they'd met. All of her questions had been answered. And now she had to start asking them all over again.

"You guys did a beautiful job hanging these," Rosanna said, gesturing to one of her portraits on the wall. It was of an older woman on a beach chair. She was wearing an oversize sun hat and holding it steady with one hand, shielding it from the ocean breeze.

"That one's my favorite," Hazel heard herself saying. It was true; she'd seen the painting in the studio and had loved it right away.

"Really?" Rosanna asked happily. "That's Adele. She's easy to paint. Her face is so expressive."

Hazel looked back at the woman in the picture. Rosanna was right. It was as if an entire catalog of emotion was playing across Adele's features. There was surprise, and even a bit of fear, maybe on account of the sudden gust of wind, but also a hopeful longing in her eyes, as if she were missing someone she hadn't yet met.

"It's like a story," Hazel said abruptly. "You've captured a moment, but there's a whole story behind it. Her story. It's beautiful."

Hazel looked quickly back at the carpet, feeling suddenly embarrassed that she'd said so much. She could feel Rosanna's eyes moving from the painting to the top of her lowered head.

"I came by your room to drop off some more clothes this morning," Rosanna said, and Hazel swallowed hard. She didn't know what excuse Jaime had given for missing work, and worried they'd be caught in mismatched lies.

"I saw some Polaroids on your bed," Rosanna went on. "Are they yours?"

Hazel exhaled, quietly relieved that Rosanna wasn't interested in an alibi. "Oh," she said, remembering the few shots she'd snapped of the gardens from the cabin window. "Yeah. I guess I forgot to put those away."

Rosanna nodded. "You have an incredible eye," she said, giving Hazel's elbow a gentle squeeze. "Have you shown your photography professionally before?"

Hazel felt a small smile breaking up her face. "Professionally?" she repeated. "They're Polaroids. I just like to mess around."

Rosanna's smile slowly faded and she let her hand fall from Hazel's arm. "That's too bad," she said. "I was hoping to include some of your work in my next show."

The cheese plates slid on the tray and Hazel lurched forward to keep them steady. "Oh," she stalled. "I don't know, I mean, I've never . . ."

"Think about it," Rosanna said, turning to wave at a pair of older men in sand-colored suits at the other end of the hall. "Just five or six of your favorites. The ones you think represent you the best. Let me know if you change your mind."

Rosanna started down the hall to greet her friends. Hazel watched as they praised Rosanna's paintings, allowing herself for just a moment to imagine that it was her own work hanging on the walls.

The tray was heavy in her hands and she started back up the stairs. *Her own work.* It sounded so pretentious and formal, and a far cry from the silly snapshots she usually took. Who would ever want to buy a picture of a shoelace?

Hazel shook her head, shoving the thought to the back of her mind. She had other things to worry about, like the tray full of cheese in her hand. Not to mention Jaime, her real mother, who was waiting for that tray, impatient as ever, and toe-tapping at the top of the steps.

16

"Y ou can let us off here," Luke called out from the back of Craig's truck. There were so many paintings at the show, and so many of Rosanna's staff working there, that multiple rides to and from town had to be arranged in order to get everybody home.

Luke and Hazel had caught the first shift and were squeezed in the back of Craig's silver pickup, sandwiched between stacks of unsold canvases. It was the first time Hazel had ever traveled in the open bed of a truck, and after she'd gotten over the initial fear of tumbling out, she'd started to enjoy the constant rush of the wind on her face. It felt good to be out in the crisp night air, and even better to take a break from thinking about the day's bizarre events.

"Are you sure?" Craig asked from the window as Luke hopped over the truck's back door. After he'd thudded to the ground, he reached out a hand to Hazel and helped her step carefully over the edge. "What about the paintings? I can take you all the way to the house."

"Are you kidding?" Maura teased from the passenger seat. "It's a miracle he even let us drive him this far."

Craig shrugged and Luke and Hazel waved good-bye from the side of the road. Luke had dragged an armful of paintings out of the truck and was struggling to walk with them tucked against his side.

"Can I help?" Hazel asked, reaching out a hand.

"No, I think I—" Luke started, but was interrupted by two or three canvases sliding down the side of his leg. Hazel grabbed them just before they hit the gravel driveway. "On second thought," Luke said, smiling, "that'd be great."

Hazel hoisted two of the smaller framed paintings beneath her arm, and they started down the narrow road that led to the estate. Overhead, a canopy of trees huddled around them, their leafy tops blinking in the cool light of the moon.

"I hope you don't mind walking," Luke said, over the hollow crunch of their feet on the gravel. "Sometimes I forget that not everybody likes it as much as I do."

Hazel smiled. The other morning, as she was leaving the guesthouse with Jaime for work, she'd seen Luke at the far end of the driveway, walking by himself. And she remembered the day she'd met him, in the ice-cream shop. He'd said he'd walked to town then, too.

"You walk to work every day, don't you?" Hazel asked.

Luke nodded. "I know, it's nuts," he said, almost ashamed. "At first I just did it because I didn't have my license, and I hated putting people out for rides. But now it's pretty much my favorite part of the day. It's quiet, and I see all kinds of things I'd never catch if I was in a car."

Hazel stared at their feet on the gravel, hearing Luke's

words echo in her mind. It was exactly how she felt about taking pictures. Looking through a lens was the only time she felt like she was really seeing what was around her, even if it had been there all along.

"And Maura was right," Luke continued. "I was totally planning on walking all the way home tonight, too."

"Why didn't you?" Hazel asked, switching arms to get a better grip on the canvases.

"I don't know." He shrugged with a sheepish grin. "I saw you getting in the truck. Figured it'd be an easy way to force you into hanging out."

Hazel smiled. Force her? Ever since she'd made a fool of herself at the bar, Hazel had been scheming ways to get Luke alone again. If she could just be herself around him, she hoped, maybe they could start over and pretend the whole bonfire freak-out had never happened.

But now that it was just the two of them, she didn't know where to start. What did *being herself* even mean? Maybe she should just keep pretending they were cousins. It had definitely been easier to talk to him when she thought they were related.

An exposed branch snaked across the road and Hazel's toe stuck beneath it. She tripped forward, taking a few halting steps before regaining her balance and scrambling to keep the paintings from crashing to the ground.

"Easy," Luke laughed. "It's not a race."

His voice was light but Hazel wanted to disappear. Her blood burned in her veins and she wanted so badly to say something normal. But the only thoughts racing through her mind were of the decidedly not-normal variety:

Sorry about running out on you before; I thought we were cousins.

Or:

I haven't been born yet.

Or:

Guess what? Jaime's my mom!

Her head was spinning and she felt the beginnings of frustrated tears springing to her eyes. Luke stopped and leaned his load of paintings against the base of a knotted tree.

"Hold up for a minute," he said, reaching out for her canvases and adding them to the pile. "I want to show you something."

Luke ducked between a pair of spindly evergreens, holding back the lower branches so Hazel could step safely through. They followed a footpath out to a clearing at the very edge of a cliff. Not far in the distance, Hazel saw the lights on at Rosanna's house, the shadow of the barn, and even the porch light of the guesthouse twinkling against the blue-black night sky. Above them, a tapestry of stars sparkled in space. And ahead, the endless ocean, stretching back and disappearing into the curtain of darkness hovering at the horizon. It felt like the end of the earth.

"Isn't it incredible?" Luke asked, sitting dangerously close to the cliff's edge. An oddly shaped rock dislodged at Hazel's feet and fell heavily toward the ocean. It slipped into the water and was quietly swallowed by a set of hungry waves.

"It always reminds me of being out on the boat," Luke mused. "It feels kind of like flying, too."

"Yeah," Hazel breathed timidly. She'd never been a fan of heights. Roy even teased her about closing her eyes whenever they drove over the Golden Gate Bridge. Slowly, cautiously, she lowered herself to the cliff beside Luke.

"It's okay," Luke joked, grabbing her knee in the firm grip of his hand. "I've got you."

Hazel smiled and felt herself slowly relaxing. Somehow, it was true. She did feel safe around him.

"Listen," he said after a moment of quiet. "I know why things have been kind of weird. So don't worry about it. Okay?"

Hazel's stomach wrenched and she dug her fingernails into the damp cracks between the rocks. "You do?" she asked, her voice shaky and small. Had he seen her in the dress by the pond? Had he found Posey's letter? Did he think she had escaped from a mental institution?

Luke took a deep breath and clasped his hands together in his lap. "Jaime told me," he said finally. "I know that she's pregnant. And I know you've been helping her out."

Hazel stared at a shimmering swath of moonlight reflected on the ocean's glassy surface. She felt immediately relieved that she wouldn't have to try (and, no doubt, fail) to explain herself. But she was also shocked that Jaime had confided in Luke about the baby.

"She told you?" Hazel asked. "When? I didn't think she wanted anyone to know."

Luke shrugged. "I've known Jaime since we were two years old. We took baths together," he said simply. "Believe me, I know more about that girl than any guy should."

"Oh," Hazel said quietly. "I didn't know." She was glad that she wouldn't have to keep the big secret alone. And she felt warmer toward Jaime all of a sudden. If Luke had been friends with her for so long, how bad could she be?

Luke kicked his feet gently against the rocks and looked

down at his hands in his lap. "She also told me that she thought it was pretty decent of you to go with her to the clinic today, but that's just Jaime for you," he said, glancing sideways at Hazel. "It wasn't just *decent*. It was really, really great."

Hazel's face flushed and she quickly looked away.

"And I just wanted you to know, I totally get it if you just want to be friends," he said gently. "Either way, I'm really glad you're here."

Hazel smiled. She felt her heartbeat rocking in her ribs. She turned to Luke and saw that he was looking straight at her.

"For Jaime," he stammered suddenly. "I mean, I'm glad you're here—"

Before Hazel had time to talk herself out of it, she was leaning toward Luke and brushing his lips with her own. She stayed pressed against him for a moment, tasting the salty warmth of his skin, before she pulled herself away.

Luke's face was frozen in a stunned half-smile, the sea breeze rustling his light brown hair.

"For Jaime," she finished for him.

Luke laughed, his strong hand finding her own in the dark.

Beneath them, the waves rolled in and pulled back out, a steady crash followed by the rhythmic drag of pebbles against the shore. Hazel looked up at the diamond-studded sky. She'd never imagined that her first *real* kiss would be under a blanket of stars, against the sound track of the open ocean, legs swinging at the end of the earth. In fact, she'd never really imagined it at all. But that was probably okay.

There was no imagining in the world that would have felt half as good as the real thing.

17

azel stood outside the ice-cream shop, an unsettled feeling in the pit of her stomach. Rosanna had sent her into town to run a few errands, and on her way home she'd decided to visit Jaime at work. It seemed like a good idea at the time, but now she was having second thoughts.

She and Jaime hadn't had a chance to talk since the opening the night before—it was late when Luke walked her back to the guesthouse and Jaime was already sleeping. Hazel had tossed and turned, every so often catching a glimpse of Jaime, wrapped like a mummy in her patchwork quilt, the rhythm of her soft, steady breathing the only sound in the room. Sometime during the night, in the dreamy, muddled space between awake and asleep, everything began to look different. Everything *was* different. Jaime wasn't the stubborn roommate Hazel had to endure. Jaime was her mother. And all of a sudden, Hazel didn't feel angry. She didn't feel upset. She felt lucky. She'd been given the one thing she'd always wanted.

She'd been given a chance to get to know her mother.

Not that she thought it was going to be easy. It was a new day, and the trip to the clinic already seemed like a scene from some faraway past. And now, here she was, stopping by unannounced to remind Jaime that it wasn't. What made Hazel think that Jaime would be happy to see her? Just because Hazel suddenly had a reason to want to know Jaime, didn't mean that Jaime had any interest in letting herself be known.

Hazel shut her eyes and leaned against the glass. She was working through a few deep breaths when Jaime appeared and plopped down on the curb at her feet.

"I can't do it anymore," Jaime grunted. "It's like the DMV in there. You'd think people would be in better moods. It's an ice-cream cone, not a parking ticket."

Hazel smiled. It was a surprising relief to hear Jaime sounding like herself.

"What are you doing here?" Jaime asked.

"I was in town for Rosanna anyway," Hazel said. "Just thought I'd say hi."

"Hi," Jaime grunted, picking at a sticky trail of drying ice cream near her elbow.

"Do you have time for lunch?" Hazel tried. She hadn't fully thought this plan through, and she knew she'd have to think fast. Maybe food would help.

Hazel craned her neck sideways and spotted a pizza place on the corner, a long line already snaking out into the street. "You should probably eat something, you know."

She started off down the sidewalk, stepping out of the way of a group of college-aged kids all wearing slightly different versions of the same maroon-and-gray UMASS T-shirt.

"Hold up," she heard Jaime call from behind her. "No way. No. No. No. Absolutely not."

"Absolutely not what?" Hazel asked, stopping to turn around.

"You will absolutely not mother me through this," Jaime said, emphatically crossing her arms at her chest. "If I wanted a cheerleader, I would've told Rosanna."

"What do you mean?" Hazel asked. "I was just asking if you wanted to eat."

"I will eat, when I'm hungry," Jaime retorted. "Just because I have a . . . thing growing inside me doesn't mean I will suddenly forget how to be a human being."

Hazel didn't know what to say. *A thing?* A baby wasn't a thing. *She* wasn't a thing. And she was only trying to help.

"Fine," Hazel sighed heavily. She realized that any time she spent with Jaime was going to have to be on Jaime's terms. But Jaime's terms were better than no terms at all. "What do you want to do?"

"For starters," Jaime said, pushing herself off the curb and striking out in the opposite direction. "I want to get as far away from this place as possible."

Hazel hurried to keep up, following Jaime to the dock and along the harbor, lined with outdoor cafés and noisy moped rental shops. Mostly they walked in silence, but every so often Jaime pointed out the best place to get fried clams, the greasiest pizza, and the tourist traps with the ugliest T-shirts and most outrageously overpriced souvenirs. Eventually, they landed back at the main intersection, just outside the carousel that Hazel had stumbled upon during her first wayward walk through town.

"The Flying Horses," Jaime said proudly. "It's the oldest carousel in the country."

Jaime took the wide front steps three at a time and Hazel followed, the dense, buttery smell of popcorn greeting them at the open doors. Inside, the carousel was a whir of colors and noise, circus music and children's squeals spinning out in waves from the rotating platform.

"The idea is to get the brass ring," Jaime explained, gesturing to a long, metal arm reaching out of one shingled wall. As the carousel spun, riders on the outer ring of horses reached out toward it, grasping for rings and dropping them onto a small silver pole spiking out of the horse's long mane. Some people would just grab one ring, while others would attack the opening with hungry, agile fingers, hooking three or four in one go.

"I think my record was seven at a time," Jaime said, beaming. "I haven't been on it in forever."

"Let's go," Hazel suggested, surprising herself. She'd never been on a merry-go-round. The only other time she'd had the option was on a trip to the county fair, organized by the group home she'd lived in for a year outside of Santa Rosa. The other kids had gone crazy over the carousel, but Hazel couldn't see the point. It went around and around and around, in the middle of a dusty, abandoned soccer field, as whiny country music played out of a boom box on a folding chair nearby.

For some reason, she knew right away that this would be different.

They waited in a winding line and soon were mounting their horses. Jaime was in front, on a tan-and-brown horse with polka-dot markings. Hazel's was a swirl of purples and pinks, its mane full and blond.

The carousel lurched forward and Hazel lunged for tight fistfuls of her horse's coarse yellow mane. Slowly, it gained speed, until it was the world around them that blurred in Hazel's vision. She watched the figure of Jaime up ahead, catching brief flashes of her face when the horses turned just so. Her dark curls flew behind her and her eyes were wide and glowing. She looked exactly like she did in the photograph on Rosanna's wall. Like there was nowhere else on earth she'd rather be.

Hazel tried to copy Jaime's movements, but she was too prepared, overthinking her alignment and missing the dispenser completely.

Finally, she figured out a way to wait until just the last minute and use her first three fingers to sift through one ring at a time. By the time the redheaded kid standing at the ticket counter announced that the brass ring had been released into the dispenser, Hazel was up to four rings every turn.

The riders became more serious as the carousel swung through its last few turns, their faces strong and determined as they reached for the rings with everything they had.

And then it was over. The ticket taker loped over to the feeder arm and swung it back against the wall as the carousel cranked to a slow stop.

Jaime threw one leg over her horse and steadily zigzagged back to where Hazel was trying to dismount without falling off the platform. Jaime held the bottom of her black-and-white Cups 'N' Cones T-shirt out like a basket, handfuls of rings bulging out of the sides. "Not bad, right?" she asked, before pointing to Hazel's overflowing piles of rings. "You have to throw these back."

She tossed her head in the direction of a giant cloth bin,

where a crowd of people had gathered to toss their rings inside, with echoes of tinny clatter. Jaime looked back at Hazel's horse. "Hazel?" Jaime spoke slowly, shaking her head. "See that ring at the top of your pile? The one that's darker than the others?"

Hazel looked back up at the top of her stack and nodded.

"That's the brass ring, you moron," Jaime laughed. "You won!"

🦋 🦋 🦋

The prize for winning the brass ring was one free ride, but Jaime didn't have much time before she had to be back at work. Hazel was pocketing the stamped voucher when she found Jaime waiting for her on the steps outside, with two fat lobster rolls crowding a paper plate on her lap.

Hazel felt a small twinge of victory and smiled—Jaime had decided to eat something after all—but she knew better than to say anything.

"Sit," Jaime commanded as Hazel hovered behind her on the wooden steps. Hazel settled down beside her and Jaime held up the plate. "Prepare to have your mind blown."

Hazel reached for one of the rolls. It was a standard white-bread hot dog bun oozing with orangey-pink lobster meat, dotted with tiny slices of celery ribs, and held together by globs of creamy mayonnaise. "Careful," Jaime warned, stretching the plate out closer to Hazel's lap. "It's sort of a two-hand situation."

Hazel brought the soggy roll to her mouth and bit down at one end. A mouthful of buttery, lemony goodness greeted her, and she swooned. "S'good," she mumbled, wiping the corners of her mouth. It wasn't just good. It was heavenly and tasted exactly the way she'd always thought that summer should.

"Yeah, it's all right," Jaime said, and shrugged between bites. "The ones on the docks in Menemsha are better. But that's a field trip for another day."

Hazel reached for one of the napkins Jaime had tucked under a sweating can of Sprite. They ate in silence for a few moments, every so often shifting closer to the railing, conceding the steps to the would-be riders bounding inside.

"I guess I *will* kind of miss this place," Jaime sighed suddenly, angling her roll to get a clean, full bite. She said it as if they'd been in the middle of a conversation, one that Hazel hadn't been aware they were having.

"Where are you going?" Hazel asked, unable to mask the interest in her voice. It escaped all in one breath, a jumbled, high-pitched squeal.

Jaime shrugged again. "I can't stay here," she said. "When Rosanna and Billy sell the farm, I'll be out of a job *and* a place to live."

"What about your family?" Hazel asked. She'd never heard Jaime mention anything about where she came from. Most of the time, it seemed like she'd been with Rosanna forever, and the rest of the time, Hazel got the impression that it wasn't okay to ask.

Jaime rolled her eyes. "Family?" she huffed. "Let's see. There's my *mom,* but she's been in India since I was four. Looking for Buddha or the perfect lotus flower or some crap."

Hazel hung on to Jaime's every word. She had a grandmother, she realized suddenly. An absentee grandmother, far away and wandering around Indian temples, but a grandmother nonetheless.

Jaime waved her sandwich in the air, little pieces of lobster meat flying onto the steps. "Or maybe you mean my *dad*. I could call him, but I'd have to make sure to get him between about eight and eight thirty in the morning. That's basically the only time he'd be sober enough to remember my name."

Jaime shook her head. "I'd also need to know where he was living. Last I heard, he was sleeping on a friend's couch behind a gas station in New Bedford."

Hazel swallowed hard and glanced down at the wooden steps. Jaime's mom had left her, and her dad was a drunk. It wasn't exactly her own story, but it was pretty darn close. Maybe it was true what people said about apples not falling far from their trees. If these were Hazel's trees, what did it say about her?

She looked back at Jaime. "How did you end up with Rosanna?"

"My grandmother," Jaime said. Her eyes warmed and all of the bitterness in her voice had suddenly dissolved. "I lived with her in the tribe until I was eleven."

"The tribe?" Hazel asked curiously.

"We're Wampanoag," Jaime explained. "Native Americans were on the island first, too, just like everywhere else. There's a reservation up in Gay Head. Don't worry, it's on the agenda."

Hazel nodded, trying to focus on chewing in slow, even bites. But her stomach had roped into a pretzel and she was suddenly terrified of choking.

If Jaime was Wampanoag, then *Hazel* was Wampanoag, too.

"She was an artist, like Rosanna," Jaime went on. "She made the quilt that's on my bed."

Jaime wiped a few crumbs from her lap. Hazel looked over at her, remembering her first day on the island, when Jaime had caught her snooping around their room. Jaime hadn't yelled at her just to be mean. She'd yelled because the quilt was special. It was the only family she had left.

"Anyway, she and Rosanna were friends," Jaime continued. "And Rosanna promised to take care of me when Grandma died. I guess that's another good thing about this island," she said, hugging her knees to her chest. "Even when you don't have a family, it finds you one."

Thoughts were crowding Hazel's brain. It was as if a dam had been opened and questions were pouring out. But there was one thing she was most curious about. It was the only possible explanation for how she could be part Native American and still have auburn hair, blue eyes, and skin so pale that it practically glowed.

"What about the, um . . . father?" Hazel managed. Her mouth was dry and she could hear her pulse drumming deep inside her ears. "The baby's father, I mean. Who is he?"

Jaime balled up the rest of the napkins in one fist and chucked them toward an overflowing trash can on the corner. The napkins bounced off the metal rim and fell to the pavement.

"I mean, you have a boyfriend, right? Emmett said . . . ," Hazel prodded. She knew she shouldn't be so nosy, but she couldn't help it.

"Technically, yes," Jaime sighed, and stood slowly, leaning over the railing to pick up the crumpled napkins. "Reid. But I haven't seen him since he visited a few months back. And there's not much he can do now, from across the Atlantic."

Hazel's mind swirled, her pulse pounding even harder. Her father. Reid. She had a father named Reid. Who was he? What was he like?

"What's he doing there?" Out of all the questions she wanted to ask, it seemed the least suspicious.

Jaime sighed again and ran her fingers through her wavy dark hair. Whatever she was thinking about looked like it hurt. "He's working at a soccer camp in England," she said, and paused before adding a sad little laugh. "Excuse me, *football*. He's going to play at Dartmouth in the fall. I thought we'd at least have this summer together, but I guess it was an opportunity he couldn't turn down."

Hazel watched as Jaime stared off at the noisy traffic, bottlenecking at the intersection out front. She was clearly somewhere else.

"He's coming back, though, right?" Hazel asked. The hope in her voice was transparent.

Jaime shrugged. "I don't think so," she said. "He's a summer kid. Which I guess means I was just a stupid summer fling."

Something changed in Jaime's expression and she looked quickly at her watch.

"Crap," she said, pulling herself up and hopping to the sidewalk. "I have to run. Ice cream for the masses and whatnot."

"Wait," Hazel started. She wanted to know more. So much more. She knew there would be time to ask all of the questions brewing inside her, but she'd already been waiting eighteen years. Once she started, she couldn't stop. "Where are you going to go? I mean, after they sell the farm?"

Jaime grabbed the wooden railing and swung back, her thick curls falling away from her shoulders. "If I know Rosanna, and believe me, I know Rosanna, there's no way she'll let me do anything but go back with them to California." Jaime shrugged. "It's why I've been putting off telling her. That, and the whole cheerleader thing."

Hazel swallowed hard and leaned closer to Jaime at the

123

railing. "What about the baby?" she asked quietly. "Do you know what you're going to do?"

Jaime rested her head in her chin, her small dark eyes seeming suddenly far away. "Not really," she said, scratching a swollen bug bite at the corner of her elbow. "I mean, I'm having it, if that's what you're asking."

Hazel nodded. She felt relieved, which she knew was silly. Of course Jaime would have the baby. Hazel had already been born.

"But I'll probably have to give it up," Jamie went on. "I'm not exactly mother material, in case you haven't noticed."

Jaime laughed, a harsh little chuckle that didn't sound real. Hazel forced a tight smile, as Jaime threw up her hands and started down the block.

"We'll see," she said. "I guess it wouldn't be the worst thing in the world, living in San Francisco," she continued, turning over her shoulder. "We could be neighbors or something."

Hazel gulped and leaned back against the steps. "Oh," she managed. "Right."

"See you at the house," Jaime called from the crosswalk with an arm in the air, and Hazel lifted her hand in a tentative wave.

How was she supposed to do this? Just sit back and watch as Jaime made her decisions one by one, decisions that would determine a specific course of events, decisions that would ultimately lead to abandoning Hazel in a San Francisco maternity ward? Not only did it seem impossible, it seemed downright unfair. She hadn't wished to meet her mother just so she could witness all of the terrible mistakes she'd made. Who would wish for something like that?

A woman in a paisley sundress was slowly climbing the steps up to the carousel. She was holding the hands of two apple-cheeked toddlers, a boy around four and a girl around two. They were both reaching out toward the painted horses as their mother crouched down to their level, tucking in their shirts and getting them ready to ride with the big kids. Hazel turned to watch the children run on their chubby little legs, weaving between the crowds and clapping their hands in the air.

She thought back to where she was at that age. Wendy had been gone for a few years. Roy had just given her up for the first time, checking himself into rehab and leaving Hazel with his elderly mother. Roy's mother was a nice old lady, but had terrible arthritis and couldn't get up the stairs very well. Hazel's earliest memories were of standing in her crib early in the morning, wailing for somebody to come pick her up.

Some days, nobody ever came.

Here, things would have been different. If Jaime found a way to stay on the island, Hazel would have a chance at a totally different life, a life full of ice-cream cones and carousel rides and lobster rolls on the beach. Even if Rosanna left, there was something about the energy on the island that made it hard to believe that Jaime wouldn't be okay. The island would take care of them, just as it had taken care of Jaime before.

Something deep inside of Hazel clicked, and she hopped up to her feet. She'd wished to get to know her mother, but that could've meant a lot of things. She could've met Jaime any time, any place. Maybe there was a reason she'd been sent back to the time before all the decisions had been made. And maybe it wasn't to simply sit on the sidelines and watch.

Maybe she had been sent back to make a difference.

Maybe she had been sent back to make things right.

18

"Are you sure you want to do this?" Jaime asked, lying sideways across her bed.

It was Saturday afternoon and Hazel was already late. The night before, she and Luke had gone for a walk on the beach after dinner. They'd been sitting on the cliffs as the sun went down when his mouth started to twitch. It looked like he wanted to say something but couldn't find the words. Finally, he told her about the Fourth of July party on Saturday night that the yacht club hosted every year. And then he asked her to be his date.

She'd said yes, of course, though the idea of making small talk with stuffy yacht club types had been tying her stomach in knots all day. And Jaime wasn't helping.

"What do you mean?" Hazel asked from the closet. She was standing in a towel, her wet hair heavy on her shoulders, as she angled Posey's second dress away from the hanging garment bag.

"I mean, I hope you're prepared for a serious snob fest."

Jaime swung her short legs over the side of the bed. They hardly even touched the ground. "And I *really* hope you're not hungry. Public eating is a major faux pas at these things. You'll probably only be able to sneak a carrot stick or two. Maybe an olive, if you're lucky."

Hazel hung the dress on the back of the closet door. Even being near it made her skin tingle. Ever since she and Jaime had talked on the carousel steps, Hazel had had a vague idea of how she wanted to use her second wish. She knew that if she could find a way to make Jaime stay on the island, she would eventually decide to keep her baby, and Hazel would have a shot at changing the past.

But it seemed like a lot for one wish. Should she wish for Jaime to stay? But what if she stayed, and still gave the baby up? Maybe she should wish for Jaime to keep her, regardless of where they went. But what would Hazel's life be like then?

The options seemed endless, and endlessly complicated. She knew that wherever the wishes led her, it couldn't be any worse than the childhood—if you could call it a childhood—she'd been stuck with the first time around. But now that she'd been given the chance to start over, she wanted to make sure she got it right.

"What's the deal with the dresses?" Jaime asked suddenly, and Hazel's stomach clenched.

"No deal," Hazel murmured. She felt her cheeks flush and flipped her head upside down, reaching for a towel and rubbing it over her damp hair. "They're just dresses."

"Yeah, but you were wearing that one the other night," Jaime pressed. "And the green one when you got here. And why do you keep them in a bag all the time? Are they expensive? They *look* expensive."

Hazel rolled her eyes, still upside down and facing the door. She suddenly longed for the time when Jaime hardly talked. The new Jaime sure asked a lot of questions. "No," she insisted. "They weren't expensive. Somebody gave them to me right before I came here."

She was amazed at how certain she sounded. It was the truth, after all. She just didn't mention the whole time-traveling, wish-granting-fairy part. No biggie.

Hazel flipped her hair back and pulled the dress off the hanger, stepping into the skirt. "Can you hook me?" she asked, and heard the bed frame creak as Jaime stood on top of her mattress, reaching up to the back of Hazel's neck.

Hazel ran her hands over the cool material as it skimmed over her hips. She held her arms out and spun around. "What do you think?"

Jaime's face brightened, and for the first time since Hazel had known her, she actually smiled. "You look like a fairy freakin' princess," she said, and kicked the closet door closed, revealing the full-length mirror hanging on the wall behind it.

The dress was just as stunning as Hazel remembered, and even more so now that she had the perfect excuse to wear it. The rose-colored silk was elegant, yet summery; it was just the right dress for an outdoor party. It was almost as if Posey had seen into the future—or the past—and designed it specifically with the yacht club event in mind.

"I can't believe you're going to waste it on Luke," Jaime joked. "I've told you he sucked his thumb 'til he was seven, right?"

Hazel laughed, lifting the hem of the dress to tuck her feet into a pair of Rosanna's sandals. There, in exactly the same spot as it had been on the first dress, was the small, embroidered butterfly.

"What's that?" Jaime asked, folding forward to get a closer look. Hazel quickly let the skirt fall and held the material close to her side.

"Nothing," she said quickly. "Just a tag."

Jaime pushed back on her bed and settled in the nook where the two walls met, crossing her legs and falling back into her pile of pillows.

Hazel spun around again, admiring her dress in the mirror. She couldn't stop thinking about the wish. When would she make it? What would she say? She only had two wishes left; she couldn't afford to screw this one up.

Jaime reached over toward the nightstand between the two twin beds. She lifted a plastic-covered book from a lopsided pile and flipped it open in her lap. It was one of the pregnancy manuals Hazel had checked out of the library the day before. Hazel's heart stuck as she remembered standing in line, wanting to shrink or disappear, and feeling like a total degenerate. The librarian had looked up quickly with a puckered little smile, and Hazel could feel herself being judged.

Poor Jaime, Hazel thought. For Hazel, the judgment had only lasted two minutes. Jaime would get it for another nine months, and possibly a whole lot longer than that.

There had to be a way that Hazel could make things better. There had to be something that would make Jaime happy. Maybe even something that would make her excited about having her baby and staying on the island to raise it herself.

An idea hit Hazel, fast and fully formed, and she glanced quickly through the closet. She pushed aside the garment bag, revealing Jaime's one sundress and snapping it free of the hanger.

"Come on," she said suddenly, tossing the white dress over Jaime's outstretched legs. "We don't have much time, and you still need to shower."

"What?" Jaime mumbled, not looking up from her book. "What are you talking about?"

"You're coming with us. I don't have time to argue," Hazel said with such force that she could hardly recognize her own voice. "And you smell like donkey. Go. Shower. Now."

🦋 🦋 🦋

"Oysters 101," Luke announced. "Watch and learn."

Luke, Hazel, and Jaime were stationed at the long buffet on the yacht club porch. The clubhouse, an old, square building that overlooked the Edgartown harbor, was lit up by red, white, and blue blinking lights, and the sprawling balcony was dotted with flags and looped with patriotic bunting.

The crowd was a sea of seersucker suits and frilly party dresses, the women lightly pecking each other on powdered cheeks, the men swirling highballs and patting each other heartily on the back. Inside, the walls were hung with black-and-white photographs, formal shots featuring boats and boaters of generations past. Hazel looked around the balcony and sighed. She couldn't help but think that Jaime had been right about the snob factor.

But she'd definitely been wrong about the food. The buffet was stocked, and hardly ignored. Guests helped themselves to plate after plate of the beautiful fruit salads, fresh greens, and steaming ears of corn on the cob. And, at the far end, there was a raw bar, an endless display of steamers, oysters, and clams, all shucked and arrayed between lemon wedges and small bowls of dipping sauce.

Luke selected two oysters and passed the smaller one to Hazel.

"Sorry, Jaime," he said, as she filled her plate with grilled chicken and salad. "No raw shellfish for you."

Jaime shrugged and poured herself a glass of sparkling apple cider. "Being pregnant is a blast," she sighed, eyeing their glasses of stolen champagne.

"Okay," Luke said, dotting their oysters with a squeeze of lemon juice, and a healthy dollop of red cocktail sauce. "Here we go."

In one quick motion, he tipped back his head, held the shell up to his lips, and sucked back his oyster in one slurpy gulp.

"So simple, so good," he sighed with a sly smile. "Your turn."

It was a challenge. Hazel looked carefully at Jaime, who urged her on with a wiggle of her thick, dark eyebrows. Hazel was still stuck on the *raw* part, not to mention the slippery way the creature was lolling around in its knobby shell. But she knew Jaime and Luke wouldn't leave her alone until she'd at least tried one.

She closed her eyes and rested the edge of the shell on her lower lip, angling the oyster into her open mouth. It was cool and wet on her tongue, at first giving her a jolt, but as it slid down her throat, it left behind a salty, fresh aftertaste, and she was surprised to find that she almost enjoyed it.

"What do you think?" Jaime asked.

Hazel smiled. "Not bad," she said with a casual shrug, as if she swallowed living things every day. "It tastes like the ocean."

"That's my girl," Luke laughed, wrapping an arm around her shoulder.

Hazel took a small sip of her champagne as they started down the porch steps and onto the club's private beach. A dance floor had been roped off in the sand, and a four-piece brass band was playing on a makeshift stage by the entrance. Luke waved hello to somebody he knew from work, and Jaime was caught in a laughably awkward conversation with one of the caterers, a stoner guy she knew from school. It was the perfect chance for Hazel to excuse herself.

"I'll be right back," she whispered to Luke, and made her way back to the clubhouse, as if in search of the bathroom. But at the last minute, she ducked around the porch, making sure she couldn't be seen from the dance floor.

Hazel leaned against the railing, the crinkling paper streamers sticking to the side of her dress. Her heart skipped. She knew this wish was risky. It could go a million ways. Or maybe it wouldn't even work at all. But she had to give it a chance. If she did nothing, Jaime was definitely going to go back with Rosanna to San Francisco, where she would have her baby and then give it up.

And Hazel's life would be exactly the same.

Hazel squeezed her eyes shut. The wind tickled her face; the air smelled like ocean and charcoal smoke from the grill. She gripped the railing and took a deep breath.

"I wish," she whispered quietly. "I wish my father was here. Right. Now."

Hazel snapped her eyes open and looked down at the hem of her skirt. All of a sudden, she felt a familiar fluttering and watched as the tiny, golden butterfly flapped its delicate wings, floating away from the dress and into the sky.

The butterfly hung in the air for a moment, as if to orient itself in new and unfamiliar surroundings, before zipping off and flying between two wooden beams on the porch. Hazel hurried down the balcony steps and onto the beach, following the glowing light as it skirted along the water.

She walked slowly between the small groups of partygoers, their pointy high heels sinking them deeper into the thick sand. She followed the butterfly's path overhead, until it paused at one of the yacht club's long, wooden piers. On the other end of the dock, Hazel could see the hunched-over shapes of Jaime and Luke, sitting with their feet in the water. Luke had sneaked a bottle of champagne and was holding it on his lap as they looked up at the stars.

The butterfly was leading her back to them.

Hazel's teeth were clenched so tightly her jaw was starting to ache. She took another step toward the dock but stopped when she felt something—or someone—brush against her arm.

"Excuse me," a soft voice uttered politely, before continuing past her and heading for the dock. He was a tall young man in a white button-down with the sleeves rolled up, and he was making his way to the end of the pier.

Hazel looked up and saw that the butterfly had swooped down and was flapping its wings with greater intensity directly over the boy's head. It traced a quick figure eight in the sky before striking out across the water and disappearing into the last of the orange sunset clouds, hovering at the horizon.

19

"**I** 'm sorry, but I'm going to have to confiscate that bottle."

The boy stood at the end of the dock with his arms crossed, speaking in a phony, official-sounding voice. Hazel had followed him quietly, her heart thudding in her ears.

Luke turned first, glancing sheepishly at the stolen champagne on the deck, before a look of surprise scrambled his face.

"Reid?" he stuttered, and Jaime whipped around, leaping up and knocking over the glass of cider by her feet. Her eyes were glowing as she hurled herself into the boy's outstretched arms.

"Reid!" she squealed, her tiny arms squeezing around the back of his neck. "What are you doing here?"

Hazel felt warm from head to toe, watching her parents hug. This was her mother. This was her father. They were together. *He'd come back.*

Jaime unpeeled herself from Reid's embrace, her face reddening as she remembered they weren't alone. She glanced over Reid's shoulders and caught Hazel's eye. "This is Hazel," she said, gesturing quickly behind the boy's back. "She works with us at Rosanna's."

The boy turned and reached out a hand. For the first time, Hazel got a good look at him. He was tall and thin, with a long nose and strong jaw. His eyes were light blue and his hair a dark auburn.

In other words, they could have been twins.

"Hi," Hazel stammered, reaching out her palm and feeling Reid's fingers wrap around hers. "It's really nice to meet you."

Reid smiled. "You, too," he said. "I'm sure Jaime's told you all kinds of horrible things about me. It's why I came back, actually. To defend myself."

Jaime punched him lightly on the shoulder, as Reid and Luke high-fived over her head. "I thought you were out of here for good," Luke said.

"I thought so, too." Reid shrugged, letting a hand slip around Jaime's waist and pulling her back in to his side. "I made it through the first session, but it got too hard to stay away."

Jaime rolled her eyes and bumped him playfully with her hip, but her face was glowing. Hazel caught her eye and smiled.

The boys chattered on about their summer plans, their voices blurring as Hazel stared at her father. Reid. She'd never known anybody named Reid before. It sounded important, like the everyday alter ego of a superhero. Her father, the superhero.

She could get used to that.

From the beach, the brassy sounds of the band wafted in their direction. An announcement was being made, and Luke glanced up.

"The fireworks should be starting soon," he said, reaching for Hazel's hand. "And I was promised a dance."

Luke led Hazel off the dock with a knowing wink. Reid yelled something about meeting up with them later, and Hazel turned and watched as he and Jaime got smaller in the distance. They were sitting at the edge of the dock, Jaime with her head on Reid's shoulder. Even from far away, she already looked like a different person. She looked unmistakably happy.

When they reached the sandy dance floor, Luke spun Hazel out and pulled her back in. Her dress swished around her ankles and she felt the strong warmth of his hands on her back.

"Did I tell you how beautiful you look tonight?" Luke whispered. The band was playing something up-tempo and festive, but they were still slow dancing, and Hazel didn't care.

"Only like seventeen times in the car," Hazel laughed. She glanced out again over Luke's shoulder toward the dock. She wasn't sure which was more startling. The fact that her parents, her actual parents, were snuggling up together, less than a hundred yards away, or the fact that a boy she liked had said she looked beautiful. Seventeen times.

"I was starting to think Jaime was never going to come out of that funk," Luke said, following Hazel's gaze. Reid and Jaime were dancing now, swaying under a sky full of prickly stars. Reid was hunched over, his knees bent and his long arms wrapped around Jaime's small waist.

"Reid seems nice," Hazel said. "Have you known him long?"

Luke shrugged and spun her around again. "Not really," he said. "His parents are members here. I used to think he was just another stuck-up summer kid. But Jaime seems to really like him. And she's not exactly easy to please. . . ."

"Yeah," Hazel laughed. "I've noticed."

Luke laughed and spun Hazel out a few more times, their

bodies settling into the comfortable rhythm of moving so close together. She couldn't believe how easy it was, letting herself relax in his arms.

The song ended and people around them stopped dancing to applaud. A sharp crackling noise popped overhead and Hazel looked up to see an explosion of lights in the sky. The fireworks had begun.

"You guys mind if we watch with you?" Reid appeared behind them, Jaime's arm tucked into his elbow. "It's getting dangerous out there." A trickle of white sparks fell from the sky toward the water.

The four of them found a long bench on the sand and squished side by side. Hazel took a seat between Luke and Jaime.

Bursts of red, white, and blue shocked the sky above them, and Hazel felt Luke squeeze the top of her shoulder. She turned to him and smiled.

"Happy summer, Hazel," he said, and leaned in to give her a kiss.

🦋 🦋 🦋

Later that night, after the fireworks and champagne toasts, Hazel had her very first sleepover.

It wasn't the boy kind. And it wasn't the first time she'd shared a room, of course. There had been plenty of nights with Jaime before that one. Not to mention all of the many roommates she'd had in the group homes, or the various step-cousins she'd been forced upon over the years.

But this was different.

When they got home, Hazel and Jaime hurried to change into their pajamas, no longer taking special care to face the wall or strategically cover themselves as they undressed. They brushed their teeth at the same time, giggling as they took turns spitting into the sink. And then they turned off the lights and jumped into bed.

Hazel watched as Jaime pulled her grandmother's quilt up under her chin. The room was dark, but just enough moonlight fell through the open window for Hazel to make out the permanent smile on Jaime's face. She looked like a completely different person, as if her features had been rearranged and softened. Hazel suddenly felt bad for disliking Jaime so much at first, when she'd been going through all kinds of complicated things. Things that Hazel hadn't had a clue about.

"Tonight really happened," Jaime said softly now, her eyelids low and heavy. "Didn't it?"

Hazel smiled in the dark. "I hope so," she said, rolling onto her side.

"You know what Reid told me?" Jaime asked. Her eyes popped open and she stared up at the ceiling. Every so often, her legs shook beneath the blanket, as if she were too excited to lay still. "After the fireworks, when we were sitting on the beach. He said he thought about me all of the time. He said it was like a piece of him was missing when we weren't together."

Jaime's voice was dry and hushed, like she still couldn't believe the girl Reid was talking about was her. Hazel knew exactly how she felt.

"I had no idea he even liked me that much," Jaime said. "I mean, we had fun last summer. And when he visited this spring. But I thought for sure that was it. I thought when he went to Dartmouth in the fall . . ."

Jaime sat up and faced Hazel, wrapping her bare arms around

her knees. "I just never thought things would work out like this," she mused. "I guess I didn't want to get my hopes up."

Hazel smiled in the dark. She'd made the perfect wish. Having Reid back was going to change everything, for all of them. Jaime would have her baby on the island and she and Reid would raise it together. Hazel rubbed her feet together, unable to lie still.

"Jaime?" Hazel asked suddenly, perched on one elbow. "Have you thought about when you're going to tell him? About the baby, I mean?"

Jaime rolled over on her back and stared up at the ceiling, exhaling a full, heavy sigh. Hazel hoped she hadn't ruined the moment.

"Not yet," Jaime said softly. "But I'll know when the time is right. I just feel like everything's happening this way for a reason. Like all of my wishes are coming true, or something. I know that sounds crazy. . . ."

Hazel closed her eyes and rested her head back onto her pillow. "No," she whispered through a smile, her voice slurred with sleep. "It doesn't sound crazy at all."

It was close to three in the morning when the girls finally drifted off, not because they'd run out of things to say, but because they were too exhausted to go on saying them. Hazel lay awake a few minutes longer, listening to the soft sounds of Jaime's breathing.

And then Hazel slept like she'd never slept before, like she'd been on a long, rambling journey, and was finally back in her own bed, heavy limbs finding familiar spots on a warm mattress. Home, home at last.

20

"Can you please stop fidgeting?" Hazel asked Luke with a laugh in her voice.

It was Saturday, a few weeks later, and Jaime's first full day off in almost a month. She'd woken Hazel up early, scrounging around her dresser drawers for a swimsuit, and insisting that it was their one chance for a double date to the beach. Luke and Reid didn't need much convincing, and after a standoff in the crowded parking lot of the most popular beach in Chilmark, the foursome had set up blankets on a secluded patch of soft white sand.

Reid was already throwing himself against the head-high waves, Jaime had gone for a walk along the red clay cliffs looming large behind them, and Luke was fidgeting on a towel while Hazel attempted to take his picture.

"I'm not fidgeting," Luke insisted, leaning dramatically back on his elbows and turning his sharp jaw from side to side. "I'm just trying to give you my good angle."

Hazel rolled her eyes and pulled Luke back up to sitting.

"I don't need your good angle," she sighed. "I need you to sit still."

Ever since Rosanna had offered to include some of her "work" in the next big show, Hazel had been trying to decide what kind of photographs to take. Clearly, she couldn't submit the types of random, cavalier shots she usually ended up with. If she wanted to impress people, and be a *real* artist the way Rosanna was, she'd have to try a new approach.

Which was when she'd remembered the portraits. The expressive face of the fisherman in the studio, the story in the old woman's eyes. What better to hang next to Rosanna's paintings of the important people in her life than photographs of the important people in Hazel's?

And, for better or for worse, she'd decided to start with Luke.

"Now, please, stop moving," Hazel begged, and Luke folded his knees, affecting a studious stare. "Just look out at the water, and pretend you see something that scares you."

Luke turned to Hazel, his sandy eyebrows raised. "What? Why?"

"Come on," Hazel insisted. "If I want Rosanna to put my stuff in the show, it has to be good. Can you please take this seriously?"

Luke cleared his throat and turned back toward the ocean. Hazel brought the lens to her eye and focused Luke's face in the frame. She watched as his brow became heavy, his light brown eyes narrowed and concerned.

"Nice," she said softly. She pressed her finger on the button, and just as she snapped the shot, Luke's eyes popped open, his jaw dropped, and he screamed.

"Shark!" he shouted. "Everybody out of the water!"

Hazel dropped the camera to her lap and spun to face the ocean. The waves were breaking right on the shore, and beyond them, the water was clear and flat and decidedly shark-free. Reid was the only one swimming, and he was either less gullible than Hazel, or had been too busy dodging the incoming waves to hear Luke's phony cry.

Hazel looked back at Luke, who was grinning mischievously, his star-shaped dimples twitching in place. "Sorry," he said, and shrugged. "I was trying to find my motivation."

Luke nuzzled his head playfully against Hazel's neck as she flapped the wasted picture dry. She tried not to smile but failed.

"Hey, Blondie," Jaime called from behind them. Hazel turned to see her crouched by the edge of the red clay cliffs. "Come here. I want to show you something."

Hazel pushed herself up to her feet, lightly kicking sand onto Luke's towel as she passed. "Thanks for your help," she deadpanned, tucking her camera and the drying photo in her bag and walking up the beach. Maybe her luck would be better with Jaime.

Hazel walked to the edge of the cliffs, where Jaime was huddled in the sand, the thick straps of an all-black racing suit peeking out of the top of her oversize Boston Celtics T-shirt. Hazel had tried to get Jaime to wear a two-piece, but she was convinced that Reid would notice the slightest thickening that had settled down around her hips. She still wasn't ready to tell him about the baby, and she didn't want to take any chances of him finding out on his own.

"Check this out," Jaime said, tracing a patch of the rock

wall with one hand, as Hazel settled next to the cliffs beside her. "If you look carefully, you can find all kinds of things in here." Her voice was wistful. "My grandmother used to take me on walks here all the time."

Hazel squinted at the dark crevices hidden in the sandy rock wall. "What are we looking for?" she asked. It all looked like dirt and pebbles to her.

"Anything that seems out of place," Jaime said, and shrugged. She ran her hand along a curve of the wall and pulled it back, her dry palm covered in a thin layer of crumbling red mud. "Some people think the clay is healing. But I just like to see what's hidden inside."

Hazel studied Jaime's face as she carefully surveyed the surface of the cliffs. Every day with Jaime was new and surprising. Since Reid had come back, there'd been a lightness to her, a sense of fun that hadn't existed before. Even when they worked together at Rosanna's, she was more patient, and less neurotic about getting everything done. And even though she'd been spending the majority of her nights off with Reid, on dinner dates in town or hanging out at his house, every night before bed she and Hazel would rehash the events of the day. It was like having a sister, or exactly like what Hazel had always dreamed having a sister would be like.

Only, in that dream, her sister wasn't also her mother. But most of the time, Hazel didn't think about that. She'd been having too much fun to think about much of anything, really, except that everything was going so well. And if it continued to go well, and Reid and Jaime stayed together, then maybe, when Jaime had her baby, they would keep her and raise her themselves. If things worked out the way Hazel hoped, she'd have nothing but more good times to look forward to. Maybe for the rest of her life.

"Look!" Jaime gasped, scraping away at layers of sand and pulling out what looked like a small, triangular rock. "It's a shark's tooth."

Jaime opened her hand and Hazel peered inside. The tooth was delicate and cracked, with little black lines running across its jagged, flaky surface. "There are tons of these in here, and they're thousands of years old," Jaime said, closing her fingers tightly around the artifact. "Arrowheads, too. It's like an entire history of the island is frozen in time. All you have to do is look for it."

Jaime's eyes looked far away and Hazel wondered what it must be like to feel so connected to a place. To have a history built inside the very earth that you walked on every day. More than just family, it was a history of a people. Jaime's people.

Now Hazel's people, too.

Hazel reached into her bag and pulled the camera out again. Without thinking, she trained the lens on the tooth in Jaime's open hand. Jaime's fingers were crusted in clay and sand and the jagged white tooth blinked between the creases of Jaime's palm.

The camera spat the image free, and it wasn't until Hazel had it in her hand that she remembered she was supposed to be taking portraits.

"Don't move," she commanded, and took a few careful steps away from where Jaime sat.

"What are you doing?" Jaime asked, folding the shark's tooth into her small palm.

"Just pretend I'm not here," Hazel said, squaring Jaime's

face in the lens. But Jaime quickly buried her head in the sleeve of her T-shirt, just as Hazel snapped the shot.

"I look like a whale," Jaime huffed as she escaped to another section of the cliffs, farther down the beach. "Not every moment has to be preserved for posterity, you know."

Hazel sighed and stuck the photo in the pocket of her bag. She didn't need to look at the blurry image to know that all she'd gotten was a blur of pink fingers and dark hair.

"Nice camera." A voice spoke suddenly from over Hazel's shoulder. She turned to see Reid standing, wrapped in a towel and dripping in the sand.

"Thanks," Hazel said, squinting up at him and leaning into his long, skinny shadow. "Too bad I can't get anyone to sit still."

Reid smiled and knelt in the sand beside her. "Don't look at me," he said, drying his hands on his towel. "I get enough of that with my dad. He's a big photo nerd."

Reid held out a hand and Hazel passed him the camera. She watched as he turned the machine over in his palms. Since he'd gotten back, Reid had spent almost all of his time with Jaime, so it was rare that he and Hazel had a chance to talk by themselves. It was easy to forget that he was so much more than just Jaime's boyfriend. He was Hazel's *dad,* and she still knew almost nothing about him.

"Is he a photographer?" Hazel asked, brushing her hair out of her eyes. "Your father?"

"He tries to be," Reid said, holding the lens up to his clear blue eyes. "He's more of a collector. He has some pretty amazing prints in his study. We should all take a ride over and see them later."

Hazel looked at her bare toes in the sand, trying to imagine the man Reid described. Her grandfather. Could it be that she'd gotten her photography-loving genes from him?

Suddenly, Hazel heard a familiar click. She looked up to see that Reid had taken her picture.

"Hey!" she whined. "Not fair."

Reid shrugged, a few drops of water dropping from the tips of his short reddish hair and landing on his freckled shoulder. "Every photographer needs to have her picture taken once in a while," he said with a smile. "How is anybody supposed to know you were there?"

Reid stood and tossed his towel to the sand, revealing his still-damp blue and white striped trunks. "Watch this," he whispered to Hazel, and tiptoed around her. She turned just in time to see him scooping up Jaime by the waist.

"Noooooo!" Jaime squealed, reaching back toward the cliffs as Reid hauled her off to the water's edge. "My shark's teeth!"

"They're just rocks," Reid laughed. "They'll be here when you get back."

Jaime pounded on his shoulders with tight little fists, her dark hair falling over her face, a wide, open grin cut from ear to ear. Reid dunked her into a wave, soaking her T-shirt and leaving her wild-eyed and laughing as she tried to catch her breath.

Hazel wiped a few grains of sand from the lens of her camera and buried it inside her bag, making her way back to the blanket.

"Don't make me come out there," Luke called from the water. He was standing waist-high in the rushing tide, waving at her to come in.

Hazel shook her head defiantly, an excited flutter already catching in her breath.

"Okay," Luke said, jogging toward her. "You asked for it."

Before she knew what was happening, Luke was there, tucking his arms around the back of her knees and tossing her over his shoulder like a rag doll. As he sprinted toward the ocean, Hazel hiccupped with delight, watching as the cliffs bounced behind them. She held her breath as the sand got darker and thicker under Luke's bare feet. Rippling white water flooded around his ankles and soon they were falling together into the shocking cold.

Seconds later, when they surfaced at the same time, they were still clinging to each other's shoulders, their noses just centimeters apart. They stayed like that for a few long moments, blinking and gasping for air, neither one of them wanting to let go first.

🦋 🦋 🦋

After the beach, after their fingers were wrinkled and pruney, their bathing suits full of sand, and their cheeks freckled and sun-kissed, Reid suggested they go back to his house for dinner.

"My parents are at some charity thing," Reid explained as they pulled out of the beach parking lot. "But I'm sure the cooks are around."

Hazel glanced at Luke, sitting beside her in the sticky backseat. *Cooks?* he mouthed, and Hazel swatted his thigh. She didn't care who was doing the cooking; her dad was inviting them to his house for dinner. She was going, and that was that.

They drove with the windows down, past working farms, lush estates, and tucked-away ponds. As Reid started to turn at an intersection near the airfield, a paved landing strip in the middle of an overgrown field, Jaime sat forward in the front seat.

"Go straight," she said, pointing through the windshield. "It's faster."

Reid continued his turn and shook his head. "I think I know the way, James," he laughed. "It *is* my house."

"Your house, maybe," Jaime said with a stubborn smile. "But it's *my* island. And you're going the wrong way."

Reid laughed and turned on the radio, flipping through static to find something that sounded like classic rock. Jaime made a face and quickly changed the station, settling on something poppier. She turned up the volume and tossed her hair to the music as Reid's eyes met Hazel's in the rearview mirror. He flashed her a bemused smile, and Hazel smiled back.

It was her first family road trip, even if *she* was the only one who knew it.

Reid turned down a side street, hugging the rocky points of the coast. The road was lined with old Victorian homes, many of which looked like restaurants or hotels. At a sharp bend, Reid pulled into a narrow driveway and turned off the ignition.

"Home, sweet home," he said as they piled out of the car. The driveway was lined with tall, manicured hedges, and a row of pink rosebushes hugged the wraparound porch.

Inside, a spiral staircase led up to the second floor, which overlooked a formal sitting room, complete with a baby grand piano and claw-footed furniture. Jaime hurried to the bathroom; she'd yet to have any of the weird pregnancy food cravings the books had prepared them for, but she was right on schedule with the constant need to pee.

"Whoa," Luke gasped, hovering over the piano and plunking a few of the higher keys. "Are you sure it's cool we're here?"

"Of course." Reid tossed his towel over a high-backed chair at the dining room table. "My parents are used to it. They're actually not as uptight as they look."

Reid lifted his eyes to a gilded frame that hung over the piano. It was a portrait of a sophisticated couple, standing in front of a glowing fireplace. The man was tall and dapper in a handsome suit, and the woman was petite with dark red hair. At their feet, two shiny-haired golden retrievers lay quietly on an oriental rug.

Hazel stared wide-eyed at the painting. Those were her grandparents. Those were her grandparents' dogs.

"Hey," Reid said, startling her from behind. "Want to see those prints I was telling you about?"

Hazel nodded and followed Reid to the stairs. Luke sat down carefully on the glossy piano bench. Hazel could tell that he was trying hard not to break anything, or drip on something expensive. She gave his shoulder a reassuring squeeze as they passed.

Reid led her upstairs, down a long hall, and through a pair of thick glass doors. His father's study was an oval-shaped room, lined with bookshelves and centered by a dark mahogany desk.

"This is it," Reid said, flipping a light switch behind the door. A dozen strategically placed light fixtures snapped on, perfectly illuminating the framed photographs that plastered every square inch of the walls.

"He's got a little bit of everything," Reid said, walking

slowly around the room. "Edward Weston, Cartier-Bresson," he listed, pointing at one shot of a group of children playing in a fountain. Hazel felt like she'd seen it before, probably in one of the coffee table books she'd spent hours flipping through at bookstores but never had been able to buy.

Hazel stood close to the pictures, slowly gliding from one to the next. She lingered in front of a tall, black-and-white image of a beach on a cloudy day, the crooked shoreline diagonally snaking from top to bottom down the frame.

"That's an original Ansel Adams," Reid said, standing behind Hazel with his arms crossed.

Hazel nodded and leaned closer, making out the title of the work. *"Rodeo Beach,"* she read aloud. "I've been there!"

She looked closer at the image of the shore. She'd been to that beach, just across the Golden Gate Bridge in Marin County, a few times with Roy, and once or twice with different group homes. It wasn't far from the city, or Roy's apartment in San Rafael, but the traffic at the tunnel was always bumper-to-bumper. Most of the time, Hazel had been forced into tagging along and was ready to leave as soon as she'd arrived. The beach she remembered looked nothing like the pristine shoreline she saw now, through Ansel Adams's lens.

"He's my dad's favorite," Reid said, pointing out a few other, similar-looking landscape views. "My dad always says the American West is a photographer's dream. I think he wishes we lived out there."

Hazel sighed quietly, looking at Reid as he crossed behind his father's desk. How many times had she wished that she'd lived anywhere else? She still couldn't believe that in a strange and accidental way, her wish had come true.

"I don't know," Reid said, stopping in front of the big bay window at the back of the room. "If I were a photographer, I'd have a hard time dreaming up anything better than this."

Hazel looked over his shoulder. The window faced the ocean and a long, crumbling jetty that wound its way out toward the horizon. A rustic white lighthouse sat atop a small, stony hill. He was right: It was a picture waiting to happen.

"Reid!" Jaime shouted from downstairs. "How do you work the TV? There are, like, two hundred remotes!"

"I'll be right there," Reid called back, starting back toward the hall. "You can hang out up here as long as you want," he said over his shoulder. "Just turn off the lights when you leave."

Hazel watched him go, his long, slender arms swinging by his sides as he hurried to the top of the stairs. "Hey, Reid," she called after him. "Thanks. This is really great."

Reid smiled. "No problem," he said with a friendly shrug.

Reid bounded down the stairs and Hazel turned back to the study. She couldn't quite explain it, but she felt somehow sturdier. As if, for most of her life, she'd just been floating around, and now she was finally attached to something real. Maybe it was the way Jaime felt about the island, and her arrowheads. They were in her blood. They made her who she was.

Hazel took one last look at her grandfather's collection, turned off the lights, and hurried downstairs to join the others.

21

"I'm out back," Rosanna called from behind the studio. Hazel was balancing two blue mugs of French press coffee in one hand and a plate of Emmett's muffins in the other. She walked carefully through the tickling blades of tall grass and found Rosanna on the patio.

"I'm supposed to be packing, I know," Rosanna sighed. It was the beginning of August and preparations for the big cross-country move were well underway. Jaime and Hazel spent most of their time packing up the office and planning travel arrangements, though they did their best to avoid talking about what any of it meant.

Rosanna was supposed to be dealing with the contents of her studio, and preparing for the end-of-summer going-away party she was planning to host at the farm. But lately it seemed like she'd been doing more painting than packing.

Today, she had set up an easel outside and was facing the section of cliff where a small cluster of beach plum trees bent sideways toward the ocean, their white flowering branches curved like icicles.

Hazel put the coffee and muffins on the low glass table and peered over Rosanna's shoulder at the canvas. She had a feeling the sudden inspiration was Rosanna's way of putting off dealing with the inevitable—the move, the realness of her disease—but wherever it came from, the result was a breathtaking collection of landscapes. She'd only just started sketching the lines of the cliffs and horizon, but Hazel could already tell she was trying something new.

"I came out here early this morning and something about the way the light was hitting the trees wouldn't let me go back inside," Rosanna said. "Sometimes when I get stuck with portraits I like to try something totally different. Kind of like clearing the slate."

Hazel looked back at Rosanna's painting. She knew exactly how she felt. After another week of failed attempts at taking pictures of her friends, she'd finally decided to go in a different direction. And since Reid had showed her his father's collection—her grandfather's collection—she'd been starting to think that maybe landscapes were speaking to her, too. Everywhere she turned was another beautiful view, and all she could hear was Reid's voice in her ear. The island truly was a photographer's dream, and she'd be a fool not to take advantage of what was right in front of her face.

Rosanna sat down in one of the wrought-iron chairs and reached for a warm muffin. "Mmmmm," she moaned, savoring a bite. "What do you think I'd have to do to get Emmett to come to California with us?"

Hazel sat on the chair opposite Rosanna and helped herself

to a crumbly chunk off the plate. Today was blackberry with white chocolate chip, the tartness of the dark berries mingling with the sweet, subtle chocolate.

"I have a feeling he'll be pretty sick of me, though, once we finish planning the menu for the party," Rosanna mused. "I told him he didn't have to cater the whole thing, but he insisted."

Hazel took a sip of her coffee and watched as a seagull swooped out over the edge of the cliff, diving for treasures in the ocean below.

"Speaking of the party," Rosanna continued, picking up her mug and tracing the faint watery ring it left behind on the glass. "Have you decided which pieces you want to show?"

Hazel swallowed a hot mouthful of coffee. "At the party?" she asked, her stomach turning an anxious flop. "The good-bye party? It's an art show, too?"

Even though the art show was always in the back of Hazel's mind, Rosanna hadn't said anything specific about it, not since they'd talked in the hotel hall. Now that it was a real thing, with a real date, and real people planning to attend, the fact that she'd agreed to participate felt real, too. Real, and scary.

Rosanna nodded. "Why not?" She smiled. "What better excuse to try and unload a bunch of paintings than a cross-country move?"

Hazel gulped and looked down at her bare feet in the grass. She'd been working hard to come up with a few solid shots, but she still didn't have anything she felt ready to show Rosanna.

"I don't know," she said softly. "I'm just not sure that anything I have is good enough. I mean, if I had my portfolio at home, the stuff my teacher used to get me into art school . . ."

"Wait a minute." Rosanna held up one long finger. "You're going to art school?"

Hazel shrugged. "I haven't really decided," she said. "But I got accepted to a program in New York."

"You're going to art school," Rosanna said again, only this time it wasn't a question. "And let me tell you one of the first things you'll learn. You're always going to be your own toughest critic," Rosanna said. "Get out of your own way, and you'll do amazing things. Okay?"

Hazel's heart swelled. Rosanna wasn't her mother, but she suddenly realized how deeply she still wanted her approval. The very fact that she was taking the time to offer advice, and taking Hazel seriously, made Hazel feel like she could fly.

Rosanna stretched her neck long from side to side, and closed her eyes. She looked tired. It was hard for Hazel to remember how sick Rosanna was. Partly because she did such a good job of hiding it, and partly because Hazel knew she had many years ahead of her. But there were certain moments when Rosanna let her guard down, and it was all Hazel could do not to reach out and hold her hand, and tell her that everything was going to be okay.

"How's Jaime doing?" Rosanna asked abruptly, her eyes still closed, the sun seeping into the shallow lines around her temples. "I hardly see her anymore. She's been spending a lot of time with that yacht club kid again, huh?"

"Reid." Hazel nodded. "They're together a lot."

"What do you think about him?" Rosanna asked. "Honestly. I've only met him once, and I haven't been able to get her alone in weeks. But she does seem, I don't know, different lately. Is everything okay?"

Hazel's heart skipped as she searched for the right words. Jaime still hadn't told Rosanna about the baby, and even though the last thing Hazel wanted was for Rosanna to take Jaime away with her to California, she couldn't help but feel like it was about time for Rosanna to know what was going on. Hazel was doing her best to be helpful, reading as many books as she could get her hands on, but she was starting to feel like maybe Jaime needed to hear some advice from somebody older.

And Rosanna wasn't the only one still left in the dark. Jaime hadn't told Reid yet, either. Lately, Hazel had been trying to drop subtle hints, hoping to figure out Jaime's plan. When was she going to do it? And how? She and Reid seemed so perfect together, and Hazel's heart leaped every time she imagined how different her life would be, if only she had grown up with them as her parents.

But first Reid would have to find out that he *was* a parent.

"Everything's great," Hazel finally managed. No matter how badly she wanted to speed the process along, she knew it wasn't her decision to make. Neither was telling Rosanna. "Reid's really sweet, and Jaime's been so much happier since he came back."

Rosanna smiled, an easy calm settling back into her clear, green eyes. "That's good," she said. "I guess that's all that matters."

Hazel swallowed hard. She always wondered what it would be like to have to lie to an adult. She used to overhear girls in the bathroom at school, putting on the makeup that their mothers had forbidden them from wearing, and relaying in hushed tones all of the stories they'd told about why they'd missed their curfews. Hazel used to think it was the one part about having parents that she wasn't missing out on.

But now, sitting across from Rosanna, she knew the other side of having to lie. It meant that somewhere out there, somebody was asking questions. Somebody cared. And suddenly, Hazel felt jealous of those girls in the bathroom. And angry, too. Angry that they had no idea how lucky they were. Rosanna wasn't Jaime's mother, either, but she cared enough to ask. And that was something.

Hazel felt more determined than ever to turn things around. If only she could grow up with a family, if only they could all stay together on the island, if only she could have a mother of her own to worry about her, to ask her questions, to make sure that she was safe, Hazel knew she'd never lie again.

22

"Hey, Annie Leibovitz."

Hazel looked up from where she was crouched in front of the barn. Her camera in one hand, she shielded her eyes with the other. Luke was leaning, shirtless and adorably bed-headed, through his bedroom window at the end of the second floor hall. "Isn't it a little early for my close-up?"

Hazel grinned, holding a finger to her mouth to shush him. It was very early morning, and she'd been trying to get some shots of the barn in the dusty, predawn light. She didn't think anyone would be awake, and had thrown a sweatshirt over her pajamas. It was a decision she was starting to regret.

Luke stage-whispered that he'd be right down. Hazel smiled and turned her camera back at the barn. She held the lens to her eye, trying to squeeze as much of the bulky red structure as she could into one shot. She liked the way the chipping red paint contrasted with the pale gray of the sunless sky, but she was having trouble deciding how to frame it.

She took a few quick shots, then turned to face the cliffs, and the ocean below. She turned a slow, half-circle, taking in the panoramic view. It was stunning, but in a way it felt like it was too much. Where would she start? Which patch of sea and sky was hers to freeze in time?

Her finger drew back the button, a few rapid snaps, as she tried to cover as much ground as she possibly could. She remembered what Rosanna had said about staying out of her own way. Maybe by starting with *quantity,* she'd stumble on some *quality* in the process.

"Ready?"

Hazel spun around to find Luke standing at the barn door. He was dressed for work, in a crisp yacht club polo shirt and clean khaki shorts.

"Ready for what?" Hazel asked, collecting her growing pile of photographs and tucking them into the outside pocket of her bag.

"You'll see," Luke said, turning on his heels and starting toward Craig's silver truck. Hazel slowly put away her camera and stretched to her feet. Her knees ached from squatting and she walked stiff-limbed to the truck.

"Hurry up," he called from the driver's seat. "Or we'll miss it."

Hazel hopped in beside him. "Miss what?" she asked. "Where are we going? And I thought you walked everywhere. Do you even know how to drive?"

"Very funny." Luke started the truck and backed out of the driveway. "And it's called a surprise, Hazel," he said, a glimmer in his big brown eyes. "The idea is you don't find out until we get there. Can you handle that?"

Hazel rolled her eyes and caught a glimpse of herself in the side-view mirror. Her hair was a mess, and she still had pillow creases on one side of her face.

"I guess I don't have a choice." She shrugged at her reflection as they bumped along the winding dirt road, and sat back to enjoy the ride.

🦋 🦋 🦋

The sky was still heavy and gray as they pulled into the yacht club's employee parking lot.

"Let's go, let's go." Luke hustled Hazel out of the truck and jogged to the end of the dock. He stopped in front of a row of small motorboats. At the Fourth of July party, Luke had explained that these were the boats he used to shuttle people out to the harbor, where they boarded their own, moored sailboats and set off on day trips around the coast.

Luke worked quickly to untie a long rope from a rusty metal cleat. Hazel thought of Rosanna's painting, the portrait she'd seen of Luke in the studio, and reached into her bag for her camera. Without a word, she knelt beside Luke's hand and focused his fingers in the frame, the slack of the rope wrapped around his forearm, the shimmering water reflecting cool, gray light in the background.

Luke smiled, shaking his head as he tossed the untied rope into the boat.

"That's the last one," Hazel laughed as Luke hopped onto the sleek bow, holding out a hand to help her jump down after him. "I promise."

Luke flipped a switch and the motor sputtered on. Hazel settled herself into the corner, watching as the glassy water slipped by the boat's rounded hull. The sky was slowly light-ening to a pale, pale blue, and they floated toward the shock of orange waiting at the horizon.

Luke tucked his knees behind Hazel's back, steering lazily with one hand. She leaned back against him, the wind picking up pieces of her hair and tossing it around her face.

"This is a good surprise," she yelled over her shoulder. The engine was loud and the wind carried her voice out over the water.

Luke leaned forward, his hair smelling like a mixture of salt and shampoo as it tickled her cheek. "We're not there yet," he said.

Hazel looked out at the harbor. They motored through the scattered rows, the massive, gleaming hulls of sailboats loom-ing large over their shoulders. Finally, when they were out in the open water, Luke shut off the engine and crawled down into the pit with Hazel.

"Here we go," he said, pointing at the horizon. He had carefully positioned them so that they could watch the sun as it slowly came into view.

Hazel tucked her head into the crook of Luke's neck. What started as a tentative burst of yellow grew into a confident ball, shocking the sky around it and throwing jewel-like pat-terns across the water's surface.

She held her breath. It was so beautiful that it almost hurt.

Luke pulled a strand of her hair back behind one ear. "What do you think?" he asked. "Still a good surprise?"

Hazel wanted to say something, but an aching sadness had settled around her heart. It was more than a good sur-prise. It was the nicest thing anyone had ever done for her.

She knew she should be happy, but no matter how wonderful and perfect Luke was, no matter how many sweet and thoughtful things he did, nothing would change the fact that she wasn't who he thought she was. He had no idea how complicated the situation was, and things were only going to get worse.

"It's a great surprise." She forced a sad smile and settled deeper into his side.

Luke squeezed the top of her shoulder. "See that boat?" he asked, pointing back toward the harbor. "The one with the stripe on the hull?"

Hazel squinted to make out the bold white script scrawled over the boat's navy blue bottom. *The Isabella?* she read.

Luke nodded. "That's her," he said, almost proudly. "The guy who owns her is a good friend of Aunt Ro's. He spends the summers here in the harbor, and every fall he leaves to sail around the world. Last year he made it all the way to the South Pacific. I keep bugging him to take me with him, but he's a real solo artist."

Hazel watched the boat's towering mast sway back and forth, the tied sails rustling in the breeze. "He travels alone all that way?" she asked.

"He used to go with his wife," Luke said, his voice softer, sadder.

"Isabella?" Hazel guessed.

Luke nodded again, his brown eyes still and serious. "She died in a plane crash when I was really young," he said. "There are pictures of her all over the club. They were the team to beat in the regatta every year. Everybody loved her."

Hazel felt Luke's hands gripping tighter around her waist.

"I guess he hasn't wanted much company since then," he said sadly.

Hazel leaned her cheek against Luke's shoulder. "Sometimes people don't know what they want until they get it," she said quietly, as if to herself.

Luke smiled, tickling her side. "Then I guess it's a good thing I don't give up easy," he said as she squirmed in his arms. "And besides, I have a plan."

"Oh yeah?" Hazel smiled. "What's that?"

"Well," he said, leaning back to stretch his long arms overhead. "Once I figure out a way to get on that boat, I can start working on getting you on it, too."

"Getting me on what?" Hazel asked, pulling back to look him squarely in the eyes.

"*The Isabella,*" he said. "You could come with us."

His voice was light and jokey, but Hazel could tell there was a part of him that was serious. The tightness in her chest was suddenly back, the unbearable clawing at her ribs.

"Why not?" Luke pressed. "Already have big plans for when the summer ends?"

Hazel stared at a murky puddle that had gathered in the corner of the boat.

"I haven't really thought about it," she said quietly, when the truth was she hadn't thought about it at all. She had managed to put a temporary block on thinking about the future. Between dealing with Jaime and the pregnancy, spending time with Luke, and working for Rosanna, it hadn't been hard to do. There was hardly time to think about next week, let alone the fall. But the future was always there, calling out from the shadows of her mind. She had no idea what she was going to do next. She had no idea what was even *possible*. If her plan worked, and Jaime and Reid decided to raise their baby together, to raise *her*, here on the island, what would happen to Hazel's life as she knew it?

But this wasn't the kind of answer Luke was looking for. Hazel cleared her throat, tucking the salty, blond ends of her long hair behind one ear. "I don't know," she started again. "I got into this school for photography in New York City, but . . ."

"You did?" Luke asked, leaning around her shoulder to look her in the eye. "That's awesome! When does it start?"

Hazel turned away, glancing back out at the blanket of endless ocean. "I don't know," she said. "I haven't really wanted to think about it."

"Why not?" Luke asked. "Because the idea of being away from me is just too awful?"

He tickled her again, and this time Hazel wriggled out of his grasp. She hadn't been thinking about the future, and now she knew why. Because if things worked out, and she got what she wanted, she'd get a chance to start her life over again. She could use her last dress and wish to go back in time, and relive her childhood, this time with happy, loving parents watching over her. But starting over would mean saying goodbye to everything she'd known before—she couldn't even keep the memories—as well as the life she was living now. And that included Luke.

"I'm just kidding," Luke teased, pulling her back in for a hug. "You don't have to think about it if you don't want to. In fact, no more thinking allowed."

Luke reached for Hazel's chin and tilted it up to his face.

She felt a burning behind her eyes and looked quickly back at the puddle in the boat.

"Hey," he said softly. "What's wrong?"

Hazel shook her head. "Nothing," she said. She wanted to tell him what she was thinking, she wanted to explain to him how she felt, but there was no way to make him understand. They could never be together. Not really.

"Whatever happens, we're going to be fine," Luke said. "We'll figure out a way to make it work. Okay?"

Hazel swallowed a lump in her throat. She didn't want to lie, but she had to. She had no other choice.

"Okay," she managed.

He hugged her closer beside him and played with a few strands of her hair, before lifting her chin to his. He pressed his lips gently against hers and she closed her eyes, trying to lose herself in the kiss. She wished she could stay here, with the sun frozen low in the sky, and never have to think about what came next. She wished she could live forever in this moment.

23

"This is a total disaster."

Jaime shook her head, squatting between two rows of strawberry plants as Hazel let herself into the garden. It was late afternoon. Hazel had been making her way back from packing boxes in the office when she'd spotted Jaime on her knees, pulling up handfuls of thick, gnarly weeds and tossing them into a pile.

"I have no idea what Maura is doing out here all day," Jaime sighed as Hazel crouched low beside her. "I swear, I heard her talking to the lettuce the other morning. How could she not notice that these poor little guys are being totally strangled?"

It was the first time Hazel had been inside the garden's mesh-wire fencing. There were rows and rows of lettuce and squash, tomato plants, grown taller than she was, tied to wooden stakes, and long, skinny pole beans casting swinging shadows out onto the footpath. The strawberry patch was tucked in a sunny spot on the far side of the garden, and was so tangled in weeds and sprouting vines that it was hard to see any of the tender red fruit poking through.

"How do you know what's a weed?" Hazel asked, gently tugging at a stringy patch of unwanted-looking green. Her fingers were stiff from ripping packing tape all day, but it felt good to be working outside.

"If it comes up easy, it's probably not supposed to be there," Jaime explained, plunging her hands into the soft dirt and dragging up fingers full of tiny green clovers. "The roots will resist if you tug on them too hard."

Hazel found a smattering of loose weeds and ripped them easily out of the earth. "Weeds?" she asked uncertainly.

"Weeds," Jaime confirmed, tossing them into the growing pile. "But look out for the runners. Strawberries are weirdos. They shoot out these long stems and root down again about a foot away. See?"

Jaime picked up a long, thick root and followed it to another smaller patch of plants, closer to the fence. "That's how you get mothers and daughters. The ones you plant are the mothers, and the ones that sprout up where the runners reroot are the daughters. And then the daughters send out runners of their own. It's like girl-only procreation. Pretty bad-ass, huh?"

Hazel smiled to herself, carefully picking around the bottom of one of the plants at her feet. There was something satisfying about pulling up weeds. It was almost like she could feel the plants breathing easier as she cleared up the crowded space around them.

"I'm telling him tomorrow," Jaime said all of a sudden. Hazel still hadn't quite gotten used to the way Jaime just picked up in the middle of a thought. She was either not in the mood for conversation or racing toward the end of one. There was never any in-between.

"Reid," Jaime continued, mistaking Hazel's quiet for confusion. "I'm telling him about the baby."

"Wow." Hazel swallowed, her heart jumping into her throat. "That's . . . big."

Hazel took a deep breath, trying to stay calm, but her pulse was beating an insistent rhythm in her veins. She'd been waiting for this moment ever since she made the wish for Reid to come back. It had been almost unbearable, and the last few times Reid had been over to the guesthouse it was all Hazel could do not to "accidentally" blurt out the secret herself. She couldn't wait until the truth was out, and they could all start planning for what would happen next. It was as if she were running a race; she could see the finish line, and all she could think about was getting there.

Jaime dusted off a tight knot of roots. She was obsessively patting the dirt around the bottom of the plant, in a way that seemed like stalling. "I think I'll tell him at Illumination Night," she said firmly. "It seems fitting, don't you think?"

There had been talk of Illumination Night all week long. Hazel still wasn't totally sure what it was, aside from an end-of-summer tradition in town involving live music, more fireworks, and lots of lanterns. Luke had asked her to go with him, as if she'd have gone with anyone else. He still got all nervous and shy about things like that, in a way that made Hazel fall for him even harder.

Now Illumination Night would be important for two reasons. A special date with Luke, before the summer's end, and the night Reid found out he was going to be a father.

"How do you think he's going to take it?" Hazel asked, forcing more calming breaths to steady the nervous tremors in her voice.

Jaime stopped weeding and stared off into the open fields. "I don't know," she said. Hazel could tell Jaime was doing her best to stay calm, too. "I really hope he's not mad at me for hiding it so long."

Hazel nodded. She pictured Reid's face, the tender way he looked at Jaime, always checking in to make sure she was okay. She couldn't imagine him ever being angry.

"And he leaves for school pretty soon," Jaime added, digging her hands back into the ground. "I have to say something if I want to go with him."

Hazel's hands froze in midair, a knotty mess of weeds clutched between her fingers. "Go with him?" she asked dumbly. She knew that Reid was going to Dartmouth in the fall. But she figured that once Jaime had told him she was pregnant, he'd change his mind and stay with her on the island. Hazel had never seriously considered the possibility that they'd go together anywhere else.

"Yeah," Jaime said. "I can't ask him not to go to college. It wouldn't be fair. And we've already kind of talked about finding an apartment together. It's supposed to be a really cool town. Lots of kids our age, tons of stuff to do, and near the mountains."

Hazel sat back on her heels. Her knees were starting to hurt from crouching for so long, and the tops of her toes were tingling. New Hampshire wouldn't be terrible, she guessed. It wouldn't be as comfortable as the island, since they wouldn't know anyone, but Reid would have his friends at school. It would be cool to grow up with young parents in a hip college town. And wherever they were, they'd all be together, and that was the important part. No more foster families that never seemed to have enough room, or on-again, off-again stints with Roy.

Hazel stared at her dirty fingernails, her vision blurring as she imagined what her life would be like. If Jaime kept her, and she and Reid raised her together, when she made her final wish to go back home, where would "home" be?

She'd have everything she always wanted. Parents who loved her, worried about her, asked how her day was over dinner every night. A real house. A real bed. Friends she'd grow up with and not have to leave behind before she'd really made them.

What would it be like? What would she be like? Would she be interested in the same things? Would she still care about taking pictures?

Or would she be a totally different person? What if she became somebody else? What if she turned into one of those ungrateful girls who complained all the time and lied to their parents? Without any idea of what her life could have been, would she even appreciate all that she had?

Yes, she decided. With a mom like Jaime, and a dad like Reid, of course she would be grateful. The three of them would be all of the family she'd ever wanted, and she'd never need to make another wish again.

"It sounds perfect," she said, turning to Jaime with a smile.

"I think so, too," Jaime agreed, though there was something small in her voice. Her thick eyebrows were knit tightly together, and the corners of her mouth were pulled in.

"What do you think you'd do there?" Hazel asked, stretching her long legs out in front of her and giving them a rest. She'd been so busy thinking about how her own life would be changing, she hadn't once thought about what it would all mean for Jaime.

Jaime shrugged and picked up another handful of weeds from the ground between her bare feet. "I'm not sure," she said. "I guess I could take classes or something. That way maybe I wouldn't feel so bad about turning down the scholarship."

Hazel paused mid-stretch and turned to look at Jaime. "Scholarship?" she asked. "What scholarship?"

Jaime reached into her pocket and pulled out a crumpled piece of paper, handing it to Hazel. "A while back, before . . . all this . . . I applied to this program that organizes digs in Peru," she said. "You know, like lost civilizations, ancient ruins, that sort of thing. It's no big deal."

"No big deal?" Hazel repeated. The letter was on thick paper with some kind of government seal, and lots of words in a language that looked a lot like Spanish but wasn't. "How long have you known about this?"

Jaime shrugged again, taking the paper back and folding it in half. "A couple weeks," she said. "But there's nothing I can do. The timing couldn't be any worse."

Jaime leaned forward and smoothed the ground where she'd been digging, tucking the plant back into the soft, solid earth. "Besides," she went on, "when I applied, I had no idea what I'd be going through. It just doesn't seem as important now that I have a family to think about. All that matters is that we stay together."

Hot tears burned at the corner of Hazel's eyes and she leaned forward to hide her face. It was exactly what she'd wanted to hear. She dug her hands back into the ground, tugging at a thick, stubborn vine. It snapped in her hand and she fell back, holding a ball of broken roots.

"Nice one," Jaime laughed in mock disappointment, tracing the root back to the mother plant. "Daughter down."

Hazel looked at the wounded roots sagging in her hands and took a deep breath, silently apologizing to the uprooted plant. She'd been there. And whatever it meant, whatever it took, things were going to be different now. She'd never have to feel so alone again.

24

*H*azel should have known there would be walking involved.

First, there was the walking *to* town, from what appeared to be the last available parking spot on the entire island. For Illumination Night, every road leading into Oak Bluffs was lined bumper-to-bumper with cars, not to mention the soccer fields overflowing with creatively parked sedans and pickup trucks. Reid, who had volunteered to chauffeur in his dad's BMW, eventually found a spot near the gas station, and Luke announced cheerfully that they'd have a bit of a hike into town.

Next came the walking *around* town, which even Jaime agreed was the only way to properly enjoy the spectacle of glowing lanterns at the center of the evening's festivities. Strings of colored paper lanterns were strung delicately from porches and hung across the windows of each of the painted gingerbread houses.

Luke led them through narrow back alleys, closed to traffic

and teeming with visitors on foot. Rows and rows of glittering houses stretched beyond them toward the ocean. Older couples sat swinging on porch chairs, holding hands and admiring the view. Every so often, Luke would wave and call out a hello.

"Is there anybody on this island who doesn't know you?" Reid asked as they crossed the street to the sprawling green of Ocean Park.

"Sure," Luke said, and smiled, his brown eyes crinkling at the edges. "But that doesn't mean I don't know them."

In the middle of the park, a swing band was playing on the wooden stage of a gazebo, and a small crowd had gathered to dance barefoot on the lawn. The sun was just beginning to set and little kids waving glow sticks ran over rumpled blankets and hopped between their parents' legs. Adults sipped wine from plastic cups and toasted another summer nearly gone by.

Luke went ahead to find a spot on the lawn, while Reid and Jaime hung back by the curb. "We'll catch up with you guys later," Reid called, grabbing for Jaime's hand.

Hazel caught Jaime's eye over her shoulder and tossed her an encouraging smile. She looked beautiful in her simple white sundress, but Hazel knew she was nervous. This was the night she was going to tell Reid about the baby. Hazel wanted to hug her friend but knew it would draw suspicion, so she held up a hand and mouthed *Good luck*, after Reid had turned to cross the street.

"Where'd they run off to?" Luke asked, swinging his backpack down over his shoulder. He pulled out a red and white striped sheet that Hazel recognized from the linen closet at Rosanna's and flapped it out over the grass.

"I think they want to be alone," Hazel said, sitting down beside him. Her stomach was in knots and she could hardly keep her mind focused on anything around her. But Luke had gone through so much trouble to make the night special. He began pulling surprises out from his bag: a Tupperware container full of Emmett's latest foray into the world of cookies (chocolate chip with pecans and dried cranberries), a thermos of pilfered red wine, and two paper cups.

Hazel crossed her legs, the grass cool and soft beneath the thin layer of faded cotton. She had agonized about what to wear. She knew she had to save her final Posey dress for later, when Reid and Jaime had a plan and Hazel could wish to start over with them, and so she'd ultimately decided on a pair of Rosanna's chocolate brown linen pants, paired with a pretty white tank with light blue flowers on the straps. As she tried to get comfortable, she was relieved she had opted against the selection of skirts Rosanna had unloaded on her that morning. (The last days of packing for California had landed Hazel with more hand-me-downs than she knew what to do with.)

Luke poured small sloshes of wine into the cups and handed one to Hazel, along with the biggest cookie in the bag. He held up his own cookie and tapped it against the corner of hers, a silly, crumbly toast.

"To a perfect summer," he said, trying to sound official as he bit into one chewy edge. Hazel smiled and did the same. The cookie was somehow still warm, and the perfect combination of soft yet substantial.

But she could hardly take more than a bite. Her stomach flipped and her heart was full and heavy. She wondered where

Jaime and Reid were right now. How would she tell him the news? What would he say?

She must've been fidgeting or making some sort of uncomfortable face because all of a sudden Luke floated his head directly into her line of vision, his eyebrows cinched and concerned.

"What's up?" he asked, before glancing down at her untouched cup of wine. "You don't have to drink it if you don't want to. I have no idea if it's good or not—it's all I could find left over at the club."

Hazel shook her head and picked up her cup. "No, it's great," she said, taking a small sip. It wasn't that good, actually, but she hardly noticed as she swallowed a tiny gulp.

The muted sounds of the band across the green wafted around them as Luke stretched out his long legs. "Hazel," he said, "there's something I need to tell you."

Hazel lifted her chin to look at him. His dimples were gone and his voice sounded different. Shaky almost, and like it was coming from somewhere deeper inside of him.

"What is it?" Hazel asked, trying to remember how many times in her life good news had followed that sentence. In the past, *There's something I need to tell you* had often directly preceded the announcement: *It's time for us to move again.* Or, the alternative, which was more common and even worse: *It's time for* you *to move again.* Whatever was coming, it couldn't be good, and Hazel felt her body shutting down.

"Just tell me," she said, her voice hard and closed. It shocked her how quickly she could switch back to the way she'd used to be. The way she'd had to be at home, always expecting to be let down, forever prepared for the worst.

"It's no big deal," Luke said, tugging at his knuckles and

176

looking at his rough, strong hands. "I just wanted you to know how much fun I've been having. You know, since you got here. Ever since I saw you in town that morning, I knew I wanted to know you. I knew it wouldn't be easy, but I had a feeling it would be worth it. And I was right."

Hazel felt all of the blood rushing to her cheeks and looked away.

"And I guess I just wanted to say, while I still have the chance . . ." Hazel felt Luke inching toward her and looked up. His mouth was doing the nervous, twitchy thing and his eyes were squinting a little bit, like he was staring into the sun. He took a quick breath and shakily let it out.

"I love you, Hazel," he said. "I love you, and I know the summer's over, and all kinds of things will be changing, but I hope . . . I guess I hope that we don't have to."

Hazel held his gaze for what felt like an eternity. His light brown eyes were still and focused, begging her to hear him, begging her to say *something* . . . but she couldn't speak.

"That's all," he said, a tentative smile pulling at his lips.

She swallowed, her pulse a stampede, echoing in her ears, and took a hearty sip of wine. Her hand was starting to tremble. She wedged the cup into the grass beside her, not wanting to spill any on the sheet. She'd heard that red wine stains were impossible to remove, probably on an infomercial for some kind of magical spray or laundry stick that you rub in circles on your shirt.

Her neck was hot, the little veins at her collarbone throbbing. Why was she thinking about laundry sticks? Luke had just told her that he loved her. He *loved* her! Nobody had ever said that to her before. No one had even come close.

She had to come up with something better than stain-lifting detergent spray.

"Luke," she said softly, looking at a spot between the red stripes on the sheet. Her eyes blurred and the crisp white lines turned pink.

She could feel Luke's body shifting on the grass as he crossed and uncrossed his ankles, clearing his throat. "What's wrong?" he asked quietly.

What was wrong? She hardly knew where to begin. Of course she loved him. At least she thought she did. From that very first day at the ice-cream shop, there had been something so easy about being around him. He was so considerate. So open and uncomplicated. And he was always *there*. He didn't disappear unexpectedly. He'd never let her down. It was more than she could say for anybody else she'd known in her life.

So what was *wrong*? She was leaving. Everything was about to change. At that very moment, somewhere not so far away, Jaime was telling Reid that they were going to have a baby. Plans were being made. History was being rewritten. A brand-new life was just a wish away. And Hazel would have to start living it.

Without Luke.

There was nothing she could say to make him understand. How could she tell him that she loved him, and let him believe that they had a future together, that things wouldn't change? How could she let him think that this was just the beginning, when it was really more like the end? It would all be nothing but a mouthful of lies.

Luke sat up a little bit straighter and turned to face her again. Hazel looked up and immediately saw the boy she'd seen from across the ice-cream shop, her very own Prince Charming. The way he'd smiled at her without even knowing who she was, so ready to give her a chance, drawing no lines between stranger and friend.

She couldn't tell him the truth. But she couldn't lie, either.

Scrambling to her feet, Hazel wiped the sides of her pants, knowing that she'd have to walk away and suddenly consumed by thoughts of crumbs and damp splotches.

"I'm sorry," she said, staring hard at the grass. "I can't."

"You can't?" Luke asked, standing up on his knees. "What do you mean you can't? I'm not asking you to do anything. I'm just telling you I love you."

He reached for her hand and Hazel pulled it away. She shifted her weight from one foot to the other. Tears were pooling in the corners of her eyes.

"What is your problem?" he asked again. Something sharp slid into his voice, and she knew without looking that his eyes had narrowed. "What are you so afraid of? I know you love me. Why is it so hard for you to say it? Why is it so impossible for you to let people in?"

Hazel's cheeks were damp and her lungs felt like they were being clenched in a vise. She wanted to be anywhere else. It felt like he was tearing her apart, reaching in and exposing all of the darkness inside of her, like a roll of film left out in the sun. She took a deep breath and looked down at him, her eyes hard and cold.

"Luke," she said, her voice strong. "The summer's over. You said so yourself. Everybody's leaving. I'm leaving. What's the point?"

Luke pulled himself slowly to his feet and reached for her

179

hands again. She couldn't keep looking at him. He was too wounded, too raw.

"The point?" he asked, disappointment dragging in his voice. "Sometimes there is no point. Not everything's about getting somewhere, Hazel. Not everything has to be a race. The point is that I love you. Isn't that enough?"

A lump the size of a tennis ball had formed in Hazel's throat and she knew she had to leave. It was more than enough. Everything she wanted was standing in front of her, her Prince Charming, begging her to let him in.

But she couldn't.

"I'm sorry," she said, pulling free from his grasp. "I'm sorry."

As she walked toward the road she felt his eyes as he watched her go, like magnets drawing her back to his side. Her head was pounding and her heart hurt.

It took everything she had not to turn around.

25

Hazel didn't know how long she'd been walking when a familiar truck slowed to a stop beside her. It was Maura and Craig. They'd had their fill of the crowds in town and were leaving early to beat the traffic when they spotted Hazel on the side of the road. Hazel got in and tried to be polite, keeping up with small talk about the plans for Rosanna's party that weekend, but really all she wanted to do was curl up in the corner and cry.

By the time she got back to the guesthouse, her eyes were near bursting from holding back tears. Hopefully, Jaime would still be out with Reid. Hazel wanted to know what happened, but she wasn't sure she had the energy to pretend nothing was wrong.

She brushed her teeth, glancing quickly at her reflection in the mirror. Her hair was longer than it had ever been, and the dyed blond ends had almost completely grown out, leaving her with her natural auburn color. Her eyes were bloodshot and hollow. Luke's voice echoed in her mind. He didn't know the whole story, but that didn't mean he hadn't been right. It *was* hard for her to let people in. But was it her fault? Nobody had ever really tried before. She'd spent eighteen years doing all she could not to get attached to anything, or anyone. What good was letting somebody in when they were only going to leave you?

Hazel splashed cold water on her face and made her way down the hall. She was opening the door when she heard the sound of ragged breathing coming from inside the room. She hurried to wipe her eyes and pull herself together.

But Jaime wasn't in any position to notice much of anything. She was hunched against the window, her knees curled up beneath her as she stared outside. She wasn't crying, but it was clear that she had been. Her face was blotchy and red, her dark eyes raw at the edges.

"Jaime?" Hazel asked quietly as she shut the door behind her.

Jaime didn't move, and for a second Hazel wondered if maybe she was sleeping. Her eyes were open, but they were so blank and still that it didn't seem possible that she was awake. She looked just . . . numb.

Hazel sat at the end of Jaime's bed, her fingers anxiously gripping the edges of Jaime's grandmother's faded patchwork quilt. The fabric was worn and the stuffing so sparse that it felt as light as a sheet, but it was somehow just enough weight to feel substantial.

"What happened?" Hazel asked, inching closer to Jaime on the bed. Jaime shrunk toward the window, as if there was a line, a limit to how close she could stand to be to another person. And Hazel had crossed that line.

Hazel leaned back and folded her legs on the bed, her bare feet dangling off the edge of the mattress. "Jaime," she said again. "You have to tell me what's going on. I'm not moving until you say something."

"There's nothing to say," Jaime whispered. Her voice was quiet and empty, and Hazel felt a chill rippling the little hairs on the back of her neck, as if a window had suddenly been opened. "It's over," she said. "I told him. It's done."

Hazel felt her throat constricting as she again tried to move closer. She didn't care if Jaime plastered herself against the glass of the window; she was going to be next to her. She had no idea what to say, or what to ask, but she knew that she could be there. That she needed to be there.

"What did he say?" Hazel asked. Jaime flinched, like the question hurt, and Hazel wished she hadn't asked it.

"What *didn't* he say?" Jaime sighed, finally blinking and settling back against the wall. "He was just angry at first. Mad that I didn't say anything sooner. I could tell just by the look in his eyes that he was terrified. All he kept wanting to know was who else I'd told, who knew, would his parents find out . . ."

Jaime shrugged and tried to laugh, but it wasn't long before what began as a loud, harsh chuckle was chopped up into little, shaky sobs.

"It's just so *stupid*," she cried, pounding the bony points of her kneecaps with tiny, clenched fists. "I have no idea what I'm even doing anymore. We were just sitting in the car, and he was talking and talking, about how young we are, about how this would change everything, about how we have our whole lives ahead of us. It was like I was trapped in some after-school special. And I was just staring out the windshield and thinking, how did I *get* here? This wasn't supposed to be my life."

Jaime grabbed both sides of her head with her hands, and all of a sudden her eyes were wild and blinking ferociously. She looked like she was being chased by something horrible, and had suddenly realized that there was nowhere left to hide.

Hazel couldn't take it anymore. She wrapped her arms around Jaime's torso, catching a combination of shoulder and elbow and squeezing tight. She couldn't believe how stiff Jaime felt, her limbs hard and taut, as if every muscle in her body was clenched and clinging to the nearest bone.

"You're going to be okay," Hazel said. She could barely hear herself over Jaime's rough breathing, her muffled sobs into Hazel's neck. But she hoped she sounded like she believed what she was saying. She had no idea if she actually did.

"Everything is going to be okay," Hazel said again. Jaime pulled back and wiped her cheeks with the back of her hands. "Maybe he just needs some time. It's a lot to take in, you know, and maybe he'll—"

"I don't think I can do it," Jaime interrupted. She was looking right at Hazel, her brown eyes darting back and forth over Hazel's face. As if the answer was there, somewhere. As if all she had to do was look close enough, or long enough, and she'd know what to do.

Hazel could feel all of the muscles in her body go slack. "What do you mean?" she asked. "Of course you can. Maybe it won't turn out like we'd hoped, maybe Reid won't be around, but . . ."

Jaime looked at Hazel like she was foreign, or disabled. A combination of sympathy, frustration, and disdain. "You don't understand," Jaime spoke slowly. "I know that I *could* do it. I just don't know if I *want* to."

Hazel reached out and gave Jaime's shoulder a strong squeeze. "Of course you want to," Hazel said. "This is your baby. *Your* baby. You're a family, now. Remember?"

Jaime rocked back and forth against the wall as she spoke, her chin bumping against her knees. She looked determined, or like she was trying to look determined. But Hazel could see something in her eyes and she knew. Jaime had already made her decision.

"I'm giving it up for adoption," she said, her voice cold and far away. "I have to."

There was a ringing in Hazel's ears and she thought for a moment that if she squeezed her head between her hands it might stop.

This is it, she thought. *This is how it begins.*

She felt her knees buckling and before she knew what was happening she was sliding down the side of the bed to the floor, landing with her legs folded in against her chest.

"Hazel?" Jaime asked. "Are you okay?"

The room spun as Hazel shook her head furiously. This couldn't be happening. It was all her fault. She had been given a second chance, and she'd lost it. She'd been sent back in the past to make things right, to make Jaime see that she should stay on the island and keep her baby. And it hadn't worked. Things were just as wrong as they'd been before.

"No," Hazel heard herself repeating, like a prayer. "No. No. No. No."

"Hazel!" Jaime was leaning over the bed, her face just inches from Hazel's. "What is wrong with you?"

It took a few moments for the words to arrange themselves in Hazel's brain, and when they did, she was able to focus her eyes on Jaime. She spun around and grabbed Jaime by the shoulders.

"You can't do this," she whispered, her voice raspy and harsh. "You just can't."

Jaime rolled her eyes, wrapping a loose thread from the quilt around the tip of her finger. "What are my options?" she asked. "I can't raise a baby by myself. It wouldn't be fair. I don't even know who I am yet."

Hazel tossed her hands in the air. "What do you mean you don't know who you are? Of course you do. You're Jaime. You're the strongest person I know," Hazel assured her. "You can do anything."

Jaime looked back at Hazel with sad eyes. "That's just it," she said softly. "I can do anything, and I've hardly been off this island. I've never even been on an airplane. I'm not ready, Hazel. You know I'm not ready."

Jaime's forehead wrinkled as she wrapped the string tighter and tighter around her finger. It looked like it was starting to hurt. "Reid was right," she whispered, so softly that if Hazel hadn't been watching Jaime's lips she may have missed it altogether. "We're both too young. I have to think about what's best for me. For my future."

Jaime took a deep breath and looked Hazel square in the eyes. "I'm taking the scholarship to Peru," she said.

Hazel felt her eyebrows lift up high in the middle of her forehead.

"Peru?" she repeated. Her head was spinning and she felt like maybe she was stuck in somebody else's bad dream. She

snapped her eyes open and shut just to make sure. "You're going to give up your baby so you can go to Peru?" she asked, once she'd confirmed that she was, in fact, awake and living this moment. "To dig up some bones, or—or shark's teeth or something?"

Jaime's finger was fading from bright red to stark white, and she finally released the thread, staring at the crisscrossed pattern of lines carved just above her knuckle.

"It's not just Peru," Jaime said, her voice getting stronger. She looked back at Hazel. "It's everything. I want my life back. I don't want this to be the last time I can do what I want to do, and not have to worry about somebody else. I want to explore. I want to be normal. Why is that so hard for you to understand? Why do you care so much what I do? This is *my* life we're talking about. Not yours!"

Hazel felt like she'd been slapped in the face, and she looked back to the floor. She slowly pulled herself to her feet, the pounding in her ears so loud she was sure Jaime could hear it. She walked slowly toward the door, then turned on her heels and pointed one long finger across the room.

"You have no idea what you're saying," she hissed. "I don't *understand*? I understand perfectly. Do *you* understand what kind of a life your baby will have after you give it up? Do you have any idea what it's like to grow up without parents? To never know who or where you came from? To be completely on your own?"

Everything around her was pulsing, cold, and strange. The room felt completely different than the one she'd spent the last two months living in. It felt like a cell.

"You've always had this island, your grandmother,

Rosanna. You can't possibly understand what that's like," she said. "But I do. I lied before, when I said my parents were traveling. I don't have any parents. I grew up in foster care. I've moved more times than I can remember. Is that what you want for your baby?"

She stared down at Jaime, who was hugging the bony points of her knees and staring at the wall. "Is it?" Hazel demanded. "Is that what you want to happen to the baby you give up? While you're out *exploring*? While you're living your life and being *normal*?"

Hazel was screaming now but she didn't care. She waited for Jaime to say something. Anything. To take it all back. To cry. To blink.

But Jaime didn't move. All of a sudden the walls felt like they were sliding on tracks, moving closer and threatening to sandwich Hazel like a paper doll between them. She scrambled for the doorknob and ran into the hall, her feet tripping over each other as she stumbled down the stairs and out into the night.

26

The ocean was angry and loud, which was exactly what Hazel needed. The sun had already set, and thick clouds of gnats buzzed around her head as she climbed down the wooden ladder to the beach. She stopped halfway and perched at the edge of a flat-faced rock, the slapping sounds of the surf drowning out her choppy sobs.

Part of her wanted to jump in. Let the tide take her away. She wanted to be washed free of the clamoring thoughts in her head. It was all too much. First, she'd messed things up with Luke, and then Jaime had decided not to keep the baby. She'd decided to do the one thing Hazel had been sent back in time to convince her not to do.

Hazel's stomach turned. If it hadn't been so empty she knew she would have been sick.

What was the point of any of this? What had she been doing here? What kind of a fairy godmother would send her back in time, just to show her everything she still couldn't have? Wasn't it bad enough that her life was such a disappointment the first time around? Did she really need to watch it unfold from the beginning?

Hazel bit the inside of her lip until she tasted blood. Her eyes burned. She couldn't remember ever feeling so full of anything. Rage coursed through her veins, her hands clenched, her knuckles white and raw.

She stood at the edge of the cliff and screamed. The wind swallowed her voice, rolling it into echoing cries for the waves to churn against the shore.

She settled back on a rock and buried her head in her hands. What was she supposed to do now? She thought of Posey's final dress hanging in her closet. She still had one wish left. But the thought of coming up with a new idea for how to use it was exhausting. She was tired of trying to fix things, when nothing she wished for made anything any better at all.

Hazel heard a rustling behind her and turned to see a little boy on the path. He was walking back from the pond, a fishing pole swinging over one shoulder. It was hard to tell how old he was, but from the way he was struggling with the tall rod and a heavy-looking metal box, Hazel guessed around eleven or twelve.

"Are you okay?" the boy asked. His round face was twisted tight with worry. "I thought I heard somebody screaming."

Hazel forced a smile and wiped quickly at the wet patches on her cheeks. "I'm fine," she said. "Thanks."

The boy shrugged, already disinterested, and turned on his heel, continuing down the path to the parking lot.

Hazel watched him go, remembering the one time Roy had taken her fishing. Even though she'd done her best not to show it, she'd been excited about the idea of catching a fish. That is, until she'd actually caught one. She still remembered the way the tug on the line had pulled her forward, and the startling sound of her own voice as she squealed for Roy to help her.

He'd been standing over her shoulders, and as soon as he'd seen the rod bowing toward the water, he'd reached out and held on to her small wrists, helping her to hold on tight. She remembered the way she'd felt, standing there with Roy's big arms looping her shoulders. Suddenly, she wasn't scared. For once, she had backup.

It was the closest the two of them had ever gotten to a hug.

Watching the boy disappear deeper into the woods, Hazel thought of Roy. Where was he now? What was he doing? Was he worried about her? Most likely he was too busy being furious. He probably assumed she'd given up on their arrangement, dropped out of school, and moved back to the city. She hadn't exactly been quiet about wanting to get out of San Rafael.

She'd never given much thought to what Roy's life might have been like, if it wasn't for her. What if Wendy had never adopted her? Maybe she wouldn't have had to work so much. Maybe she wouldn't have been at the restaurant the night it burned down.

Maybe Wendy and Roy would have lived happily ever after.

On the other side of the trees, the boy started to whistle, a clear, simple tune that carried in the breeze across the cliffs. Hazel wondered what Roy had been like at that age. What did he imagine his future would be like? Surely he'd hoped for more than he'd ended up with: a lost love, and the unwanted responsibility of a daughter he'd never asked for. No wonder he had such a hard time keeping it all together.

He really had loved Wendy. That much, Hazel knew. Somewhere at the bottom of a buried tangle of memories, Hazel could recall the muffled crying sounds she used to hear coming from Roy's room, those first, shaky years after Wendy's death. She couldn't imagine having to lose somebody she loved that way.

She couldn't imagine losing Luke.

Luke loved her. She felt it, as surely as she'd ever felt anything in her life. Maybe she hadn't just been sent back in time to meet her mother. Maybe she'd been sent back to find Luke, too. She'd never been able to get so close to anyone before. Of course it scared her, but he would understand, eventually. He understood everything else about her. How could she leave him behind?

And what was waiting for her at home, if she did? What was so great about the future that she needed to ever go back? Roy was miserable. She didn't have any friends. And what good could come out of that other life she'd started? A life of fragmented memories, of being let down. A life of reminding Roy of what he'd lost.

A life of being a burden.

Hazel took a shallow, trembling breath. That wasn't at all what she wanted. What she wanted was here, all around her. This place, this beautiful place, and all of the people she'd found here. Rosanna, Jaime, Luke.

She'd made a wish to get to know her mother but she'd gotten so much more.

She'd found her family. And she wasn't ready to leave them behind.

She thought again of her third dress, and suddenly she knew what she had to do. She didn't know how it would work; she didn't know what it would mean.

But she knew she'd found home, and she knew she had to find a way to stay.

27

"Careful with that," Rosanna called through the studio door. It was the day of the going-away party, and Hazel was helping Rosanna arrange her paintings on easels outside.

Hazel looked down to see that she had been standing in the studio with a painting balanced precariously against her knees, lost in another daydream.

It wasn't the first time Rosanna had interrupted her in the middle of a faraway thought. Earlier in the afternoon Hazel had dragged one of the handmade display easels through a puddle, trailing mud across the patio floor. She'd spent an extra twenty minutes scrubbing the dirtied stones, and though Rosanna hadn't said anything, Hazel could tell she knew that something was wrong.

"I'm sorry," Hazel said as she picked up the painting and continued carrying it outside. "I guess I'm a little bit distracted."

Rosanna was surveying the space, inching one easel closer

to another and considering the new arrangement. She smiled warmly at Hazel and nodded. "I can see that," she said. "Is everything all right?"

Hazel quickly lifted the painting in her hand. She propped it against an empty stand and prayed that it hid any telltale changes in her face. How could she explain to Rosanna any of what was going through her mind? That every time she caught a glimpse of the barn roof and thought of Jaime, she felt a twinge of guilt? She knew that Jaime could use help closing up the office and packing up the house, but she couldn't imagine the two of them spending the whole day together. Not after the way they'd left things the night before.

And there was no way Hazel could tell Rosanna what she'd decided last night as she'd sat by herself on the cliffs. How could she reveal that she was planning on using her final wish to stay in the past? Especially since now, in the clear morning light, she wasn't even sure it was possible. Whatever Jaime decided to do with the baby, Hazel would have to be born. She couldn't go on living in the past after it became her actual present, could she?

"Let's take a break," Rosanna said, interrupting her wayward thoughts yet again.

She straightened the painting and gestured for Hazel to follow her back inside the studio. Hazel's arms were starting to ache from lugging the heavy canvases back and forth across the lawn, and she was relieved to rest for a moment.

Rosanna stood in the middle of the open room, which felt big and light now that there was hardly anything in it. She pointed at the far wall, empty but for a shelf in the corner.

"I was thinking we could put your photographs there," she said. "How does that sound to you?"

Hazel swallowed. In all of the drama of the past few days, she'd forgotten about her photographs. She hadn't chosen the ones she wanted to display, or done anything to arrange them in any interesting ways. In fact, she wasn't even sure she knew where they were.

"Rosanna," she said, her shoulders tight. "I don't know if it's still a good idea."

But Rosanna just waved her off and leaned over the desk. She pulled open a drawer and removed a thick folder, spreading it open on top of the table.

"Have a look," she said, crooking a finger over her shoulder and beckoning Hazel close.

Hazel glanced down and saw that Rosanna had chosen a few of her photos and matted them together on pieces of crisp, white foam. Set apart like that, Hazel hardly recognized them as her own. They looked almost professional. They looked good.

"Wow," Hazel gasped. "I . . . I don't know what to say. . . ."

"You left these in here the other day, and I knew you were having trouble deciding, so I chose a few that I liked best. Just tell me where you want them," Rosanna said, turning back to the wall. "I've spent all day ordering you around. Now it's your turn to show me."

Rosanna walked to the wall with an armful of photographs, holding up a few at different angles. Hazel watched her, this woman who had taken her in, no questions asked, when she'd showed up at the studio less than two months before. This woman who had believed in her, for reasons Hazel still didn't completely understand. This woman who was about to leave behind the home, and the people she loved, to fight an illness she didn't deserve, and hadn't spent a moment feeling sorry for herself because of it.

The tears were running down Hazel's cheeks before she knew to expect them. She sniffed and Rosanna turned, her eyes suddenly wide and concerned.

"Oh my God," she said, dropping the photographs and rushing to Hazel's side. "What's the matter? Did I go too far? I should've asked first. I'm sorry. If you really don't want to show them we don't have to."

Hazel shook her head and tried to speak, but the sobs were choking her now, trapped in the bottom of her throat. Rosanna led her to the armchair by the window and settled her inside of it, rubbing her back in small, comforting circles.

"I always do this," Rosanna admonished herself, grabbing for a tissue from a box on the table. "I just get so excited when I see something I like. I want other people to see it, too. But it's totally up to you, Hazel. I promise."

Hazel smiled and dabbed her eyes with the tissue. "It's not that," she hiccupped. "Really. I'm happy you want to show them, I am."

Rosanna looked at her skeptically. "You look thrilled," she said, before smiling and hugging Hazel's shoulder to her side.

"It's just . . . ," Hazel began, taking a deep breath and dropping her hands helplessly to her lap. "I don't want the summer to be over. That's all."

Rosanna nodded and squeezed Hazel's arm. "I know," she said.

"And I feel terrible complaining about it to you," Hazel continued. "Because I have no idea how you're handling all of this so well. I mean, you're leaving tomorrow. You're selling the farm. You're . . ." Hazel stopped herself and looked at the floor.

"I'm sick," Rosanna said, perching on the arm of the chair. "You can say it. And you don't have to feel bad about anything. Of course you're sad about leaving. Look out there." She pointed through the window at the open lawn, the jagged line of cliffs and the blue of ocean and sky beyond them. "Who wouldn't have a hard time leaving this place?"

Hazel picked at a hangnail and stared at her fingers. "It's not just that," she whispered. "It's . . . it's what I'm going home to."

Rosanna pulled back and looked down at Hazel, her green eyes warm, urging Hazel to go on. "My parents . . . ," Hazel started, and stopped. What could she say? It was too much, and too much to ask of Rosanna to understand.

"Your parents aren't traveling in Europe," Rosanna said simply.

Hazel wriggled out of Rosanna's grasp and turned to look up at her. "You knew?" Hazel asked.

Rosanna nodded solemnly. "I had a feeling." She shrugged. "I could tell there was something you were hiding from. A past you didn't want to define you," she said quietly. "I see it all the time."

Rosanna stood and walked to the empty wall, crouching over Hazel's photographs. "But what I *don't* see all the time," she continued, "is this."

Rosanna held up a mounted Polaroid and gestured for Hazel to join her. Hazel squinted across the room, trying to recognize the image in the frame. It was a photo she'd taken of the garden, she could see that much. Late one evening, after she and Jaime had been weeding. She'd been so upset about accidentally uprooting the strawberry plant that she'd gone back to take its picture.

"Look at this," Rosanna said, bringing the photograph closer to Hazel and placing it in her lap. The edges were blurry but the center was green and focused, and the one upside-down plant, its dirt-covered roots reaching toward the sky, stuck prominently out of the bottom corner of the frame. It looked like arms stretching for a hug, or a mouth open wide, raw and sore from screaming.

"You see things that most people don't," Rosanna went on, kneeling in front of Hazel. "Small things. Stories that aren't usually told, stories that need you to tell them."

Hazel looked closer at the photograph, trying to see it through Rosanna's eyes.

"Do you remember what you said to me at my show?" Rosanna asked. "You were talking about my portrait of Adele. You said you saw a story there. But it wasn't her story. And it wasn't mine. It was yours."

Hazel remembered the look she'd recognized in the woman's eyes, and how the painting had made her feel.

"It's the same story I see here, in this photograph," Rosanna said, waving the Polaroid in her hand. "And the only reason you're able to tell this story, is because of who you are. And where you've been."

Hazel looked back at the plant in the picture. She hadn't realized it before, but there *was* something there. Something more than just a pile of dirt. It was a story. Hazel's story. And maybe it was worth telling.

"We all hit bumps on the road to where we're going,"

Rosanna said. "But it doesn't mean we're on the wrong road."

Hazel looked up at Rosanna. She reached her arms around her neck and hugged her close. She suddenly wanted nothing more than to tell Rosanna everything, if only so she wouldn't have to worry about how much time she had left.

But maybe that was the point, Hazel thought, her eyes squeezed shut and her face buried in the warmth of Rosanna's long hair. Rosanna had to travel her own road, just as Hazel had to travel hers.

Hazel leaned back and wiped the remaining tears from her eyes. "Thank you," she said. "For everything."

Rosanna smiled and nodded, before climbing carefully to her feet and starting toward the door. "How about I let you hang the rest of these?" she said. "Billy will have a fit if I don't lie down before everybody gets here."

Hazel stood and watched Rosanna go. "Rosanna?" she called, just before she'd closed the door.

Rosanna turned back. "Yes?"

"I just want you to know," Hazel said, "I have this feeling. . . . I have a feeling your road is a lot longer than you think."

Rosanna stood framed by the screen door, staring back at Hazel. Her eyes glistened and she looked like she wanted to say something, but instead she just nodded and raised her hand in a wave, before softly closing the door and making her way across the lawn.

Hazel took a deep breath and watched Rosanna disappear. She turned back to the empty wall, and looked at the mounted photographs in the folder. For the first time, she noticed a loose pile of pictures, and bent down to look through them. They were the ones that hadn't been mounted. All of her thwarted attempts at portraits, and the pretty panoramic shots she'd taken around the estate.

Rosanna hadn't chosen any of these to frame.

Hazel looked again through the mounted photos on the floor. They were all of seemingly everyday things. Jaime's shoelace, that morning they'd come back on the boat from the clinic. Luke's fingers as they worked the fraying rope. The shark's tooth in Jaime's open palm. Small, as Rosanna had said, and focused.

She'd spent so much time trying to be like other people, she hadn't noticed she had her own style, all along.

Hazel thought back to the last day she'd spent in San Francisco. The shot she'd snapped of the crooked books on the side of the road. Suddenly, she remembered Jasper. She saw his face as he admired her photograph. She remembered what he'd said about Miss Lew. They'd believed in her from the beginning. She just hadn't believed in herself.

Hazel looked back at the discarded pile at her feet. The landscapes were beautiful, but they weren't hers. They didn't tell her story, not the way the others did. The others were less glamorous and more contained, but together, they were pieces of something. They were pieces of Hazel, of where she'd been, what she'd seen and who she'd become.

She thought of home, the pieces of the life she'd left behind. She thought of Roy, and the apartment he'd kept just so she'd have a place to come back to. He'd been trying so hard, and she hadn't even given him a chance.

She thought again of Jasper. The way he was always popping up, inviting her places. The way he refused to give up, even when she gave him nothing but reasons to do so.

She though of Miss Lew, who had done everything she could to make sure that Hazel wouldn't miss an opportunity to follow her dream. Even before Hazel realized that she had a dream to follow.

They were all pieces of Hazel, pieces of her life. And maybe they were the right pieces, after all.

Hazel reached down for the picture of the strawberry plant and held it up in the center of the wall. She picked up a hammer from the table and nailed the foam board in. It wasn't until she was hunched over the picture, centering it between the wooden panels, that she noticed the root in the corner.

While most of the scene was wild and chaotic, the scraggly weeds scattered and abandoned in the dirt, in the far corner one root had already found its way back into the earth. It still looked delicate and wounded, like parts of it would always stay broken. But there was no question in Hazel's mind that there in the corner, all by itself, one stubborn root was quietly starting all over again.

28

Hazel was walking back around the main house when she spotted Jaime on the porch. She was balanced precariously with one foot on each arm of a patio chair, reaching up to the trellis with a long string of white lights. She hadn't spotted Hazel and for a moment Hazel wondered if she should just keep going. The conversation with Rosanna had left her feeling solid and prepared, but she still wasn't completely sure for what.

Just as she was ready to quietly step away, Jaime turned to bend down for a tangled pile of wires on the table. "Oh," Jaime said, surprised. "You scared me."

Hazel cleared her throat and moved out of the shade of the house. The sun felt like a warm bath on her skin, not stinging hot as it had been for the past few days.

"Sorry," she said. "Want some help?" Hazel picked up another string of lights and passed them up to Jaime, who took them in her outstretched hand.

"Thanks," Jaime said, studying the wires for a few

unnecessary seconds, before reaching back up toward the arched wooden structure.

Hazel fiddled with the lights in her hands. A thick silence hung between them.

"Jaime," Hazel started, lowering herself into one of the chairs. It was made of ornate metal and dug at the tender undersides of her legs. She shifted forward, leaning into the fabric of her denim shorts, and steadied her hands on her bare knees. "I just wanted to say—"

"You were right," Jaime interrupted, swinging the last loop of lights around the trellis and stepping down from the chair. She clapped her hands together, heaved a giant sigh, and stood with her hands on her lower back.

Sitting down, Hazel was staring directly at Jaime's belly, which had finally started to show a bit, rounding the front of her minuscule frame.

"You don't have to say anything," Jaime continued. "You were right. I was wrong. End of story."

Hazel looked up from the bump in Jaime's belly to the shadow of her face. Her arms were folded beneath her chest and she was staring fixedly at the wooden planks on the porch. Her dark eyes were unblinking and her small mouth was pinched and severe.

Hazel smiled. Jaime was trying so hard that it almost hurt to look at her.

"Jaime," Hazel said. "You don't have to do this. I was—"

Jaime waved her hands in the air between them and slowly settled herself on the ground, sitting cross-legged. "Stop," she said. "It's done. I don't know what I was thinking before. I can't do it. You're right, it wouldn't be fair."

Hazel shook her head, ready to interrupt, but she felt her

breath becoming shallow again. She knew it wasn't right, what Jaime was proposing, but hearing her say the words out loud still made Hazel's heart ache with possibility.

"I thought about it last night," Jaime continued. "I thought about what you said. About how you never really knew where you came from or who you were. I can't be responsible for somebody feeling that way. I thought I could go through with it. I thought I'd be okay. But I won't. I can't. I just can't."

Hazel swallowed the lump that reappeared in her throat. "What about the scholarship?" she managed to ask quietly.

Jaime shrugged. "I can apply again later. Just because I'm having a baby doesn't mean that my life will be over."

Hazel watched as Jaime absentmindedly picked at the thick tufts of grass that were pushing up between the wooden floor. Her eyebrows were angled sharply toward each other, her lips still tight and pursed. She looked years older, like the idea of staying on the island, the idea of settling down before her life had even begun, had somehow aged her overnight.

It was Hazel's fault. She never should have wished for Reid to come back. He was leaving now, if he hadn't already gone, because it was what he was always meant to do. It didn't make him a terrible person—it just made him somebody not ready to be a father.

Just like Jaime wasn't ready to be a mother. Hazel stared into her friend's eyes, and suddenly saw Jaime's future, playing like a fast-motion movie across the features of her face. It was a life full of adventure and travel and following her own path.

No matter what it meant for Hazel, she couldn't ask Jaime to give up on all that.

"Jaime," Hazel started. "I came here to apologize, because what I did was wrong."

Jaime shook her head stubbornly and started to interrupt, but Hazel held out a hand.

"You were the first person who's ever been a real friend to me, and last night I wasn't being one to you." Hazel sighed. "I was thinking about myself. I wasn't thinking about what's best for you. And I'm sorry."

Jaime didn't move right away, but Hazel could see the relief settling into the curve of her friend's narrow shoulders. She stopped tugging at the grass, her eyes still and calm as she stared at a faded wooden panel, knotty circles traced like a bull's-eye on its surface.

"You have to do this," Hazel said. "You have to take that scholarship. It's what you're meant to do."

Jaime brought her hands back into her lap, her shoulders low and hunched. Hazel thought she saw a quiet quivering of Jaime's lower lip, and sat down on the porch beside her. "You're doing the right thing," Hazel said. "You are."

"What about the baby?" Jaime whispered to her hands in her lap. "How will it know . . . ?" Jaime's voice cracked and faded as she shook her head.

"Know what?" Hazel pressed, laying a hand on Jaime's shoulder.

"How will it ever know how hard this was? What if it just thinks I didn't care?" Jaime asked, looking up and meeting Hazel's eyes with her own. One perfect tear was stuck between Jaime's long, dark lashes, and she blinked it free. "How will this baby have any idea how much I love it already?"

Hazel's jaw tightened as she tried to fight back tears. She

inched closer to Jaime and pulled her in close. Jaime collapsed into Hazel's arms, heavy and sobbing, and Hazel rocked her gently back and forth.

"Trust me," Hazel said, tucking Jaime's head against her own. "She'll know."

29

Posey's third dress was all kinds of wrong.

Hazel stood in front of the unzipped garment bag, biting her lower lip and shaking her head. Somehow, in the past, Posey had managed to be so spot-on with her designs, but this time she'd completely missed the mark.

The dress was beautiful, of course, and Hazel could tell it was going to fit perfectly as soon as she pulled it over her head. That wasn't the problem.

The problem was that it was too . . . much. It was sleek, black, and very sophisticated, with elegant golden flowers embroidered on the bodice and waist. The straps were narrow and rested gently on her shoulders, and the skirt was long and fitted.

She took one look at herself in the mirror and gasped. It definitely wouldn't have been her first pick for an end-of-summer outdoor affair, but one thing was beyond apparent: She looked gorgeous.

She was still staring, dumbfounded, at her own reflection

when Jaime returned from the shower, her hair wrapped in a towel turban and her one white sundress sticking to her legs.

"Wowza," Jaime said, her jaw hanging low. "You clean up nice."

Hazel blushed and turned. "It's too much, though, isn't it?" she asked uncertainly. "I mean, for tonight?"

Jaime flipped her head upside down and vigorously rubbed at her wet curls inside the towel. "I don't know," she mumbled. "I say go for it. Give Luke something to remember you by."

Hazel tossed Jaime a look and bit her lip. "I just don't know if I can pull it off," she said, tugging at the bottom of the skirt. "It's so not . . . me."

Jaime flung the towel on the floor and squished her wet curls in the palms of her hands. "Whatever it is," Jaime said, "it works. But, here. I have an idea."

Jaime pulled out one of her dresser drawers and removed a small, suede pouch, tucked all the way in the back. She loosened the drawstring that cinched the pouch shut and reached her fingers inside.

"This should take you down a notch or two," Jaime said, pulling out a long silver chain and looping it around Hazel's neck. At the bottom of the chain was a smooth, purple shell, the shape of a kidney bean, a lopsided half-moon.

Jaime hooked the clasp and stepped back to admire the finished result. "Perfect."

Hazel touched the shell with her fingers. It was smooth as glass on one side, and rougher and ridged on the other.

"It's so beautiful," Hazel whispered, turning the shell over in her hand.

"It was my grandmother's," Jaime said, crouching down again to search for shoes on the closet floor. "She wore it on her wedding day. It's supposed to bring luck in times of change . . . or something." Jaime tossed sneakers and boots out of the way, grunting as she dug to the back.

"Jaime, I can't take this," Hazel started, but Jaime shooed her away without looking up, finally sitting up and holding a pair of black flip-flops.

"It's yours," Jaime said. "Besides, I have a hundred just like it. She was obsessed with collecting things. Guess it runs in the family."

Hazel smiled, looking back at her reflection. When she looked carefully, she could see that the inside of the shell wasn't just purple, it was layers and layers of every shade of purple imaginable, gradually fading all the way to soft white.

For a moment, Hazel could have sworn she'd seen the necklace before. But she couldn't remember where. Maybe on the beach. Or in the seashell gravel outside.

Whatever it was, she felt stronger wearing it. Like Jaime's quilt, it was a piece of their family, and Hazel knew she would carry it with her forever.

"Hey," Jaime said suddenly. "What happened to your hair?"

She was staring at Hazel's reflection in the closet mirror. Hazel smiled and flipped her long, auburn hair dramatically over one shoulder. "It grew out," Hazel said. "Guess I'm really not Blondie anymore, huh?"

Jaime flashed her a wide, cheesy grin. "Oh, you'll always be Blondie to me."

Hazel laughed and looked back at herself in the mirror, the necklace catching in the late afternoon sun. She hadn't recognized it at first, but with all of the right ingredients—her hair, her smile, the necklace, even Posey's dress—falling into place, now there was no question.

At last, she looked like herself.

❧ ❧ ❧

When Hazel got to the studio, there was already a crowd inside.

She'd left Jaime and the others in the billowing white tent set up on the lawn, and followed the gravel path, lit by a string of white lanterns. She stood outside the studio door, taking deep breaths and readying herself to go in.

It was the first time she'd seen her own photographs anyplace other than taped to a classroom wall. And even though she'd already seen them in the studio, earlier that day, there was something about the room being full of strangers that made the pictures on the wall look different. It was almost as if she could see the pictures for what they actually were. They weren't just quirky ways she'd found to pass the time. They weren't crutches, or props to help her see the world.

They were photographs, and they were pretty damn good.

But it wasn't until she heard it from a total stranger that she actually believed it one hundred percent. She was on her way back out to the lawn, anonymous in the crowd of Rosanna and Billy's friends, when she heard snippets of a conversation behind her.

"Do you know whose work this is?" one woman asked. Hazel froze, her ears straining to catch the response. It was the first time she was eager to hear that she was being talked about.

"It's a friend of Rosanna's, I think," another woman

answered. "A young girl who's been living here. They're lovely, aren't they?"

"Yes," the first woman agreed. "Whoever she is, she's incredibly talented. And I'm surprised to hear that she's young. There's a real maturity there, don't you think?"

Hazel's cheeks flushed. She pushed quietly back outside and walked over to the tent, an irrepressible smile brightening her face. She had almost reached the long buffet when a familiar voice called out from over her shoulder.

"Look at that dress!"

Before she knew what was happening, Rosanna was beside her and twirling her around.

"You look absolutely stunning," she said as Billy quickly appeared at her side. Their elbows had been knit all night long, and Hazel had watched them float from one group of guests to another, wearing brave faces as they made plans to come back and visit the island soon.

"Thank you," Hazel said quietly as Rosanna reached out to touch one of the golden flowers. Hazel was still feeling self-conscious, and felt overdressed among the summery crowd.

"There's only one problem with it," Rosanna said, tracing the back of the collar with her finger and tapping Hazel lightly on the shoulder. "It may be gorgeous, but it's a city dress."

Rosanna winked at Hazel and nestled back into Billy's side. Maura and Craig joined them at the buffet, and the conversation shifted to plans for the fall, Maura's upcoming trip to New Zealand, and Craig's dream to one day have a farm of his own. But all Hazel could hear were Rosanna's words replaying in her mind:

A city dress.

Rosanna was right. That was exactly what the dress was. It wasn't meant for the island, or even for Hazel's life in San Rafael. Had Posey known what she was doing after all?

Hazel tried to imagine herself in New York City, getting ready to go out to a swanky restaurant, maybe with candles on the tables and heavy menus and interesting art on the walls. Or maybe she'd be on her way to a gallery opening, a show of some new photographer's latest work. Or maybe, just maybe, it would be her own show, her own photographs hanging on the walls, for all the world to see. . . .

"What happened to all of the dumplings?"

Hazel turned to see Jaime standing beside her at the buffet. She was surveying the picked-over selection of appetizers, her plate already littered with toothpicks and paper wrappers. The pregnancy cravings had finally kicked in, and the buffet had suddenly become Jaime's new best friend.

"I know, I know," Jaime sighed, pulling her loose-fitting dress out farther from the hidden bulge of her belly. "I'm enormous."

Hazel laughed and shook her head. "You are not," she insisted. "You look great."

Jaime crossed her arms over her stomach and sighed. "I'm going to have to tell Rosanna soon," she whispered. "They're leaving tomorrow."

Hazel glanced to where Rosanna and Billy had made their way across the lawn, talking to an interested buyer about one of the bigger portraits.

"It's not too late to go with them, you know," Hazel mumbled under her breath. "I'm sure Rosanna would appreciate having you around."

Hazel watched as Jaime chewed nervously on the inside of her lip. "I don't know . . . ," Jaime started. "She's already got so much to deal with. I don't want to be a burden."

Hazel shook her head. "You wouldn't be a burden," she said. "You could help each other."

As soon as the words had left her mouth, she knew they would come true. Jaime would go with Rosanna and live with her in San Francisco until she had the baby. Rosanna would help her arrange for the adoption. And Jaime would see Rosanna through her treatments, helping her recover before setting off on whatever adventures the rest of her life held in store.

It was what was meant to happen, all along.

She turned to Jaime and hugged her hard. She couldn't wait for Jaime to know all the things she knew, how happy she'd be, how full her life would become. "You could take care of each other," she added.

"Okay, okay," Jaime said, peeling Hazel's arms from around her neck. "I'd say we've had enough touchy-feely moments to last us a lifetime."

Hazel smiled sadly. She hoped that Jaime was wrong. Could they maybe meet again, in her lifetime?

"Anyway, I think there's somebody else who'd like a word with you," Jaime said, lifting her chin toward the far corner of the tent. Hazel followed her gaze and found Luke, sitting alone at one of the round, carefully appointed dinner tables. He looked miserable, staring vacantly at a cheerful centerpiece of tall purple dahlias.

"I don't know what you did to him," Jaime said, shaking her head slowly. "But I haven't seen him this choked up since the summer of the big hurricane, when he couldn't go sailing for weeks."

Hazel's heart dropped and she looked down at her hands.

"What are you waiting for?" Jaime said, nudging Hazel with the point of her elbow. "Go fix it."

30

"Feel like going for a walk?"

Hazel stood behind Luke, watching as he traced dejected circles on the linen tablecloth with the end of a heavy silver fork.

"What?" He jumped and turned around. His brown eyes looked flat and sad, but brightened some when he saw her standing behind him. "Oh. I guess so," he said, pushing back his chair and following her out of the tent.

They walked in silence across the lawn, catching pieces of friendly conversation as guests milled about, gathering around Rosanna's art. Hazel was leading them back to the path and down to the beach, the same route they'd traveled on bonfire nights. She remembered back to the very first bonfire, when she'd thought they were related and left him speechless in the sand. She couldn't imagine how he'd felt then, or how he felt now. Like nothing he did was ever good enough. Like it was his fault she couldn't let him in.

They reached the bottom of the crooked staircase and

found a patch of sand to sit in, still warm from the fading sun. It was late evening and the sky was so clear that the moon was already bright, even while the sun clung to the horizon.

Hazel tucked the skirt of her dress beneath her thighs.

"That's some dress," Luke murmured without looking at her. "I wanted to tell you before, but I didn't know if you were talking to me yet."

Hazel looked down at the slippery black material of her skirt. No matter how beautiful or sophisticated it was, at that moment she would've given anything to have been wearing sweatpants instead. She was in a sweatpants kind of mood.

"Thank you," she said quietly, shivering and burying her bare feet beneath the sand.

Luke peeled his arms free of his tan blazer and draped it over Hazel's shoulders. "You looked a little chilly," he said. He was left wearing only a thin, pale blue button-down, the sleeves wrinkled and pushed up to his elbows. There was a hint of a late summer's burn peeking through at the bottom of his neck.

Hazel hugged the coat close under her chin and nodded. "Thanks," she said. "I guess I was."

Hazel stared out at the water. As usual, she didn't know where to start. She knew Luke was upset and confused. He had every right to be. She wanted to fix it, just like Jaime said. The only problem was that she didn't know how.

"I'm so sorry, Hazel," Luke said all at once, the words tumbling out like they'd been stuck together too long.

Hazel turned to him quickly. "You're sorry?" she asked. "What do you have to be sorry about?"

Luke dragged his hand through the sand, raking lines beside his kneecaps. "I shouldn't have laid all that on you before," he said softly. "It wasn't fair. You have every right not to be ready, or not feel the same way I do. . . ."

"Luke, stop," Hazel said, placing her hand over his in the sand, working her fingers into the spaces between his. "I do feel the same way. I always have. Ever since that first night, when we sat right here."

"You mean the night you ran away like I was contagious?" Luke laughed.

Hazel smiled and took a steadying breath. "Yes," she said. "And I'm sorry. I'm sorry I run away all the time. And I'm sorry I make everything so hard. But the truth is . . ."

She squeezed his hand and looked up into his eyes.

"The truth is I love you," she said with a shrug. "That's all."

Luke held her gaze, the darkness in his eyes slowly lifting. He smiled and leaned in, finding her lips with his and kissing her, soft and sweet.

"Much better," he said, leaning back into the sand and kicking off his brown loafers. He patted the sand beside him and gestured for her to lie back. She tucked herself inside the crook of his arm and looked up at the darkening sky.

"There's only one, tiny problem," he said, his chin resting on the top of her head.

"What's that?" she asked, finding his hand again and wrapping it around her waist.

"The problem is . . ." He took a deep breath and let it out slowly between clenched teeth. "I finally get the girl, and I have to get on a boat and sail around the world."

Hazel shot up, practically knocking Luke sideways and swiveling to face him head-on.

"You're going?" she asked, a smile springing to her face. "*The Isabella?* He's letting you go?"

Luke smiled and pulled her back to his side. "We leave in two weeks," he said, unable to mask the excitement in his voice.

Hazel turned her head and kissed the warm, rough side of his cheek.

"What was that for?" he asked.

Hazel shrugged and looked back out at the clear, flat water. "For not giving up," she said.

Luke crossed one ankle over the other and settled back deeper into the sand. "You know, I was kind of hoping you'd at least pretend to be mad. . . ."

Hazel nudged him with her elbow and smiled. "I can't be mad," she sighed. "Not when I'm leaving you first, to go to New York."

Now it was Luke's turn to look surprised.

"I knew it!" he exclaimed, squeezing her waist in his hands. "I knew you'd end up going. You were planning on leaving me for the big city all along."

Hazel shook her head forcefully, a playful smile on her lips.

"You totally were," he continued. "Just leave the little country boy in the dust. Moving on to better things."

Hazel rested her head on Luke's chest, listening to the steady thud of his heartbeat echoing deep against her ear. She felt the lump growing in her throat again and swallowed hard.

"Luke," she said, pulling back to look him straight in the eyes. "I may be leaving, and you may be leaving," she spoke slowly, her voice now strong and clear, "but there will never be anything better than this."

She stared into his eyes, watching as they struggled

heroically to blink back the beginnings of tears. "Yeah," he said softly. "I guess some people just meet in the wrong place, at the wrong time."

His smile faded and his mouth started to twitch, his lips pursing as he fought to hold on to a steady, calming breath.

"Hey." Hazel nudged him gently. "I have an idea. Everybody's still up at the party, right?"

Luke cleared his throat and nodded, his eyes still foggy and dazed. "Yeah," he tried shakily. "Yes, I mean. Why?"

Hazel shot him a sneaky smile and climbed to her feet. She took a quick peek at the ocean, which was calmer now, lapping at the shore in gentle, rolling waves, before glancing back at Luke, one eyebrow perched high, a challenge.

"You want to go in?" Luke asked uncertainly.

Hazel took a few more steps toward the water, feeling the cool night air tickling her legs under the hem of her dress. She reached down and tugged the skirt up, tossing Luke a quick, sly smile over her shoulder.

"Oh man," Luke said, scrambling to his feet, unbuttoning his shirt and wriggling out of his tie.

Hazel laughed as she tossed her dress up and over her head, taking a few more deliberate steps toward the ocean. She could hear Luke rustling around behind her, kicking his clothes off and hurrying to meet her. But she didn't wait for him to catch up. She looked out at the ocean, stretching back as if it might never end, as if she could swim out and just keep swimming. And suddenly she was six again, on the dock at the lake, but there was nobody behind her. Nobody pressuring her to jump. It was just Hazel and the sea, the endless sea. Scary, open, and full of possibilities.

All that was left to do was dive in.

After they swam, they slept.

Luke ran back for a sleeping bag and they spread it out at the bottom of the wooden steps. He crawled inside first, holding one side open for her, their damp limbs entwining as they huddled together to stay warm.

They stayed up late, talking, counting the stars, dreaming out loud, and planning the future.

He made her promise she'd write him letters. She said she would. She thought it would be hard to lie, but it didn't feel like lying.

She said she'd never forget him, and she meant it.

She knew she never would.

Hazel woke up with the first bird's song, her eyes blinking at the early morning sky. The cliffs were still covered in darkness, the sun just barely tinting the horizon pink and gray.

She had no idea what time it was, or how long they'd been sleeping. Luke was snoring gently beside her, his chestnut hair flecked with sand. His eyelids twitched in his sleep and Hazel thought he must be dreaming.

She didn't want to wake him. Slowly, carefully, she crawled out of the sleeping bag. In the middle of the night, Luke had wrapped her again in his jacket. Not wanting to change back into her dress, she held the coat tight around her waist.

She found her dress and balled it up in her hands, catching her flip-flops between two fingers. After a long look up and down the beach, the cliffs, the studio, and farm in the distance, she crouched down beside Luke's head.

She kissed him gently on the forehead, soft and fast. "Good-bye, Luke," she whispered into his hair. "I hope all of your dreams come true."

His eyes twitched faster and he rustled in the sleeping bag. Hazel's heart stalled. It looked for a moment like he might wake up.

But he burrowed deeper into the bag, pulling it tighter under his chin. His eyes stopped twitching and a peaceful calm settled over his face.

Hazel smiled and turned in the sand. Somewhere in the trees, the bird she'd woken up to had found a friend, and together they sang a sweet duet as she carefully climbed the stairs, leaving the beach, and Luke, behind her for good.

31

*T*he plan was to sneak out while everyone was still asleep.

Downstairs on the kitchen table, there was a folded schedule of ferry departures, and Hazel decided she'd be on the first boat. That gave her just enough time to grab her bag and start walking. If she caught a ride on the road, even better, but if she had to walk, she'd make it if she left right away.

Hazel climbed the steps in the guesthouse, careful to skip the few that creaked the worst. Pale sunlight shone through the tiny bathroom windows as she quickly changed back into her dress. The only sounds were the whooshing of water in the pipes, the occasional call of a gull swooping past. It was amazing to think that in just a few hours the place would be buzzing as everybody else finished packing and started saying their good-byes.

Hazel knew she couldn't stand to be there. To make more promises about staying in touch that she knew she wouldn't be able to keep. Better just to disappear. She'd leave a note. They'd understand.

At the door to her room, Hazel stopped, one hand closing over the wooden knob. How could she leave without
saying good-bye to Jaime? Her eyes stung and she squeezed
them tight to keep from crying.

She didn't have a choice. She knew what she had to do. She
might as well do it fast.

Hazel pushed open the door without making a sound,
spotting her bag in a heap at the end of her bed. She'd packed
the day before. All it held inside of it were the three dresses—
the original, still-torn dress that she'd never worn, the one that
had brought her to the island, and the one that brought back
Reid—her collection of photographs, and her camera. The bag
felt flimsy as she quietly lifted it up and slung it over her shoulder, and she wondered for a moment if she should even bother
bringing it at all.

It was time to go. Hazel took a few careful steps toward the
door, pausing for one last look at Jaime. She was still asleep
but had folded the blanket down from over her head. She was
facing the wall, her eyes shut, her hair still wild and free.

As soon as Hazel reached the door, she heard a rustling on
the bed.

"Hazel?" Jaime called out, just as the door was closing.

Hazel waited for a moment. It would probably be better
just to leave. Pretend she was never there. Maybe Jaime would
think she'd imagined it.

"Hazel, I can see your feet."

Hazel looked down at the crack beneath the door and
smiled. "Hey," she whispered, poking just her head back
inside. "Sorry, I didn't want to wake you up."

Jaime pushed herself up onto her elbows and squinted at

Hazel, her features scrunched together and confused. "I was just having the strangest dream," she mused, before shaking her head. "What time is it?"

"Early," Hazel said. "I'm going to try to make the first boat."

Jaime sat up all the way and leaned forward, her hair tumbling down toward the shapes of her knees, still swaddled in blankets. "You're leaving?" she asked.

Hazel closed the door behind her and sat across from Jaime on her bed. She nodded slowly. "I should get back home," she explained. "School starts soon, and—"

"I hate good-byes, too," Jaime interrupted. "I was planning on sneaking out on you, too."

"You were?" Hazel smiled.

Jaime nodded and pulled the quilt up around her shoulders. "I told Rosanna last night," she said softly. "I'm going with them to California."

Hazel smiled, a calm settling inside her. She put a hand on Jaime's shoulder, the quilt warm and soft on her skin. She imagined Jaime taking the quilt with her to California, and then maybe to Peru, the one piece of home she'd always carry with her, wherever she went. It made her happy to know that Jaime wouldn't be alone.

Without another word, Jaime fell forward and wrapped Hazel in a hug. Her body was still heavy with sleep and smelled sweet, like a baby. Hazel held her tight, fighting back the tears that were pooling in her eyes. She wanted to tell her everything. How meeting Jaime had made all of her wishes come true. Even the ones she didn't know she was making.

But she knew that she couldn't. She untangled herself from

Jaime's arms and forced a smile; then she stood and walked quickly to the door.

"So I'll see you when we get there?" Jaime asked hopefully, stretching her arms and falling back into the pillows. "To California?"

Hazel stopped at the hall. She couldn't lie again. She knew she couldn't tell Jaime the truth, but she couldn't lie anymore, either. She turned to look at Jaime over her shoulder.

"Tell me about your dream," Hazel said. Jaime was already tucked back under the quilt, curled in a tiny ball near the edge of the bed. She closed her eyes and smiled.

"Yesterday," she began sleepily, "when we were hanging up the lights for the party, you were talking about the baby and you called it a she. And ever since then, I've had this feeling you were right. I can't explain it. I just know."

Jaime reached out from under the covers and scratched the bridge of her nose with one hand. With her eyes still closed, she continued. "And last night, in my dream, I had my baby," Jaime said. She was smiling now, a small, sweet smile, and her voice was softer, her words slower and farther apart. "I saw her. I got to hold her. She was so beautiful. The most beautiful baby you've ever seen. And I named her Hazel. After you."

Hazel stood frozen in the hallway, shivers racing up and down her arms. Jaime's breathing deepened, and she was still mumbling as Hazel started to pull the door closed.

"I love you, Hazel," she heard Jaime say, just as the door was almost shut.

Hazel closed the door and stood beside it, one hand pressed against the frame.

"I love you, too," she whispered.

32

The boat was nearly empty when Hazel got on. In the booths on the lower level, a few early morning commuters slept beside their lunch coolers. Hazel felt a quick shot of envy as she walked past. How lucky they were, she thought, to get to come home at the end of the day. To get to come home here.

Hazel quietly climbed the stairs and walked past the snack bar, smiling at the woman behind the row of steaming pots of coffee. The woman wore a uniform of matching pink visor and shirt, and was picking at the crumbs of a Danish wrapped in plastic. Hazel thought about eating. Who knew when she'd have another chance? But something told her she'd be too anxious to keep anything down.

She was here for a reason.

Hazel pushed through the heavy steel door, a gust of wind forcing her to take wide, underwater-type steps across the deck.

Most of the plastic blue chairs at the front of the boat were empty. In the far corner, a man in a Boston Red Sox cap was lifting up a little boy and angling him out over the railing. The boy had a mop of dark hair and was holding out one chubby fist, clutching a piece of bread between his fingers. Every so often, a sea gull would swoop down and lunge for the bread, and the boy would squeal, tugging his hand sharply back. Finally, the man took the bread himself, and held it far above the boy's head. The little boy clapped as the gull finally scooped it up. He'd really just wanted to watch, all along.

Hazel smiled to herself as she walked down the side corridor, passing the wall of windows and finding a quiet spot halfway between bow and stern. It was a rare, crisp morning, with very little fog, and it felt like she could see all the way back to Rosanna's estate if she looked long enough. The harbor town was sleepy and still, the beach empty, the roads long and winding and with only one or two cars in sight.

Hazel swung her bag onto the railing and took out her camera. She held it up and squared as much of the island as she could get in the lens, taking a picture. When it came out, she flapped it in the breeze.

It was surprisingly warm for being so early, though she was glad to be still wearing Luke's coat. She'd meant to leave it on his bed in the barn before she left— along with the picture of herself, the one Reid had taken of her on the beach—but she'd been in such a hurry that she'd forgotten.

And she was glad to have something to cover the dress. It wasn't exactly an outfit for traveling in, particularly not so early in the day.

Hazel watched as the blurry image in the photo cleared. She heard voices calling from the dock, ropes being untied and the groaning of machinery, the engine rumbling beneath her feet. She looked up to see a patch of water growing between the end of the boat and dock. For a moment it looked like it was the island that was receding, slipping off into the ocean, floating toward the horizon.

She took one last look at the island, matching it to the image in her hand, before tucking the photo carefully with the others in her bag. She laid the bag on the ground beside her feet, and slipped out of Luke's coat. She folded it twice, laid it on top of the bag, and turned to the railing.

The island was just a strip of land now, grass and sand and tiny houses, shimmering as it sat quietly on top of the water. Hazel closed her eyes and took a full breath, the salty, sweet air filling her lungs, tickling her nose, and drying the damp, sticky corners of her eyes.

She thought of Luke, probably still asleep on the sand. And of Rosanna and Billy, waking up, enjoying their last morning at the house. She thought of Maura and Craig, getting up to feed the animals in the barn.

She thought of Jaime, and she instinctively touched the shell around her neck.

She'd wished to get to know her mother. And she had. No matter what happened, she would always have that. It was a gift, a gift she never imagined she'd be given. She may never see the island, or Jaime, again, but that wasn't what mattered. What mattered was that she'd been there once. She'd known them all for a little while.

And now it was time to go home.

"I'm ready," she whispered under her breath. "No more excuses. No more looking back. I wish to go back to my life, wherever it takes me, and whoever I become."

Hazel's heart was racing as she snapped her eyes open, waiting with her lungs full.

For a moment, nothing happened.

And then, just like twice before, the fluttering. The gentle flapping of material at the hem of her skirt. She looked down, underneath the fabric, to where the little golden tag was struggling to detach itself.

Slowly, the glowing butterfly broke free, hovering up near her face, its tiny wings beating against the air. She smiled, remembering the first time she'd seen it. How she'd thought she was losing her mind. When really, she was starting to find it.

The butterfly was still hanging in the air when a thick gust of wind swirled around Hazel's ankles, kicking up pieces of sand from the deck and whipping her hair around her face. The butterfly looked trapped, and Hazel almost wanted to reach out and save it, but the wind was too strong. It built up to a howl, scooping the little bug up and carrying it away, until it was just the faintest light, burning high above the whitecaps in the distance.

The wind picked up again, growing even stronger, and Hazel shielded her eyes with one arm. She struggled to stand, to stay by the railing, but the wind was driving her back. She staggered toward the window, burying her face against the glass, tasting the spray of the ocean on her lips. She pressed her eyes closed, her heart pounding in her ears as the wind screamed in circles around her.

A blinding white light flashed across the insides of her eyelids, and Hazel felt herself falling to the floor, gripping her head in her hands, and hoping it would all soon be over.

And then it was.

33

Even with her eyes squeezed shut, Hazel could feel the dark.

She slowly blinked them open. The wind had vanished, leaving an eerie quiet, and all around her was a darkness, more inky blue than black.

As her eyes adjusted she saw a tiny glowing light, and thought for a moment that it was the butterfly, still stuck somewhere in space. Slowly, she realized it was the twinkling of a star, as hundreds of others came into view, huddled together against the open sky.

She pulled herself carefully up to her feet, and walked out toward the railing. She was still on the side of the ship and had to crane her neck in one direction or the other to see past it. She looked behind her first and felt her stomach flip.

The mountains of Marin were fading into the darkness, the bridges hovering high and bright on either side.

Slowly, without breathing, she turned the other way, the slick blanket of ocean slipping past the hull. Ahead, she saw the lights of San Francisco, the familiar skyline, the open port.

It was home, and she was headed toward it.

Hazel looked back at the window, now recognizing the boat as the ferry to Larkspur. The one she'd gotten on, in tears, that night after learning that her mother—or the woman she'd thought was her mother—was dead.

Rosanna. Hazel's heart ached as she thought of the event, Billy inside at the bar. Rosanna was still gone. Nothing would change that.

In fact, nothing had changed at all. Hazel checked her watch. It was 9:42. And the date, months earlier, the very day she'd left. Only a few short hours after she'd first climbed on board.

What did it mean? Hazel wondered as she searched the boat for clues. Had it all been a dream?

Hazel's heart was pounding as she crouched beside the window, tearing open her bag. The pictures! She'd packed the Polaroids, all of the pictures she'd taken of the island, and her friends, the ones Rosanna hadn't framed. They were real. They had to be.

Hazel tore around the insides of her backpack, frantically trying to find the envelope. She flipped the bag over, emptying its contents onto the grated metal floor.

All that fell out was a single dress. The one she'd bought herself. The one she'd found at the thrift store, with the tear that refused to be fixed.

Hazel felt her eyes welling up with angry tears. This couldn't be happening. She opened the bag wider and peered inside. But it was empty.

Hazel leaned against the window, fighting back the

throbbing in her throat. Her breathing was ragged and frantic, and she was overcome by a sudden, queasy feeling. She squeezed her eyes shut and tried to steady her pulse, slowly pulling air in and letting it out.

"I wish to go back to the island," she said out loud, not caring who was around to hear her. "I changed my mind. I wish to go back to the island."

But when she opened her eyes, she knew it wouldn't work. The tag was gone. The last glowing butterfly had flown away.

Hazel felt an uncomfortable pain in her side and realized she was squished against something on the floor. She reached behind her back and felt a familiar scratchy fabric.

Luke's coat. She remembered taking it off before making the wish, and somehow, it was still there. She hugged it tight against her, pressing her face into the collar and breathing in his scent.

It was real. All of it. Luke, Jaime, the island . . . they were all real and a part of her now.

Hazel thought of something and flipped the jacket over in her lap. She rummaged through one pocket and then the other, her fingers finding the cool, slick photograph and angling it free.

The picture that Reid—her father—had taken of her on the beach, the wind in her hair, the faraway look in her eyes. That was real, too.

She stared long and hard at the picture, wondering why it was the only one she had left. But it was something. A reminder of where she'd been, who she'd been, before the summer that changed her life.

She tucked the photo back in the pocket and felt the familiar jolting of the boat against the dock. She looked up to see the Ferry Building, looming large overhead.

She was back where she started.

She hurried to the exit, her feet carrying her off the boat before she'd even decided it was the right thing to do. The attendant stood off to one side, announcing that this would be the final trip back to Larkspur. She should just stay on, she knew. She should just go home.

But she couldn't leave without knowing. Had nothing really changed? What would she find in that restaurant? Would Luke be there? Would Jaime?

Hazel scurried down the ramp and along the dock, still crowded with tourists taking pictures. She stood at the restaurant door, peering inside the glass, the same window she'd looked through before.

The easel was there, and on it, the same picture of Rosanna. The woman with the short, dark hair and her companion, who had been the ones to break the news to Hazel by the buffet, were dancing, swaying gently side to side. And across the room, still at the bar, still by himself, was Billy.

Hazel swallowed hard. She wanted to go inside. To go to Billy. To hug him and tell him it would be okay. She wanted to look for the others. What did they look like now? Where had they ended up? The only thing keeping Hazel from finding out was a door, a window, a single pane of glass.

But what if they didn't remember her? Or what if they did? How would they feel, seeing somebody they'd known, so many years ago? Somebody who hadn't changed a bit, while they had all grown older. While they'd moved on and lived their lives.

It would be confusing, to say the least.

And this wasn't the time or the place to explain. It wasn't

her night. This night was for Rosanna. Besides, there was a part of Hazel that didn't want to know if somehow, what had happened for her and all that it had meant, hadn't meant the same thing to everybody else.

She took one last look at Rosanna's picture through the glass.

"Good-bye, Rosanna," she whispered, and turned to walk away.

She was halfway to the bus when she realized she didn't have her bag.

She ran back to the restaurant, thinking maybe she'd dropped it, but soon remembered that she hadn't seen it since she'd emptied it upside down on the boat. She'd left it there, on the deck, with her thrift-store dress inside.

Hazel hurried back to the dock. The boat was still there, and she ran to it, willing her feet to go faster.

But just as she reached the ticket booth, the horn blew. The ropes were thrown and the boat pulled back, gliding out across the water.

Hazel's heart sunk. She'd never see that dress again.

She was about to turn around when something caught her eye on the boat. It was a figure, a person holding a child, and at first Hazel thought it was the man and the little boy from the Vineyard, holding out bread to the gulls.

But the figure turned and Hazel could see that it was a woman with long, blond hair and a little girl. Hazel took a few steps closer, shielding her eyes from the bright lights of the dock, trying to get a better look.

The little girl was reaching both arms over the railing, and Hazel recognized the little sparkling flower clips in her hair. The girl from the bathroom. The one she'd seen washing her hands. The wind picked up and Hazel could hear the girl squealing with delight, saying something over and over again. She was waving, and it sounded like she was saying, "Bye, bye. Bye, bye. Bye, bye."

Without thinking, Hazel raised her hand, too, waving back to the little girl and her mother as the boat carried them away.

The woman balanced her daughter on one hip, shaking her arm free of her shawl and raising it to join in the waving. There was a quick flash of light, a reflection from lights on the harbor catching on a dangling piece of silver around the woman's neck. Hazel felt her pulse speeding as she leaned over the wooden railing, squinting, her fingers frozen mid-wave.

It was a purple shell. The necklace. Her hand quickly traveled to her throat, and she felt the cool of the chain that Jaime had given her, the smoothness of the shell against her skin.

The woman Hazel had seen in the bathroom. The woman with the daughter.

Her hair was dyed blond, but it was still long and wavy, and the small, dark eyes were unmistakable.

Jaime.

Hazel lifted her hand again, waving, small at first and then bigger, making wide circles with her arm. She wanted to yell. To tell Jaime to come back. To beg the attendant to turn the boat around.

But no words would come.

The woman on the boat tucked her arm back inside her shawl and pulled her daughter close to her chest. They turned away and walked inside, the shape of their bodies huddled together, as they vanished into the soft, yellow light of the cabin.

34

The next morning, Hazel woke up slowly.

It took her a few moments to remember where she was. A bright, dappled square of light hit the floor by her bed, and she could see through the window that the sun was shining, breaking between the folds of the green and white curtains. She was in her bed, on her old, lumpy futon, back in San Rafael.

She was home. It was spring. And finally the rain had stopped.

She lay still and closed her eyes again, replaying the night before. Her bag on the boat. Billy at the bar. Rosanna's picture in the frame.

Jaime.

She sat up with a start. Had she really seen Jaime on the boat? It had been so dark, and she was far away. It could have been any necklace.

But, no. It *had* to be her. She looked the same, except for her hair. Hazel smiled. Jaime was the Blondie now. She'd looked older, of course, and happier. Exactly the way Hazel had seen her when she'd imagined what the future would bring. Full and assured of where she'd been and where she was going.

Where *was* she going? Hazel wondered. Did she live nearby? The ferry was the only boat to all of Marin County. She could have been traveling anywhere. But was it possible they had been neighbors all along?

Hazel remembered the little girl, the one she'd seen in the bathroom, and then again on the boat. Jaime's other daughter. Hazel's half sister.

Before, the idea of her birth mother having another child— and keeping her—probably would have made Hazel angry, filled her with the burning jealousy she felt whenever she thought about all she'd missed out on.

But now, as she pulled herself out of bed, ready to start her day, she didn't feel any of that. She'd been exactly where she needed to be, done all of the things she'd needed to do. And she was her own person because of it. She hadn't missed out on anything.

Hazel got dressed. She wondered what Jaime was doing at this very moment. She knew it wouldn't be impossible to find her. She imagined herself at the computer at school. All she'd have to do was type in Jaime's name, Marin County, maybe try each of the different towns. With a few quick searches and the press of a button, Hazel could be reunited with her mother by the end of the day.

But it didn't feel right. She didn't know what it was, and she couldn't say how long it would last, but she felt, deep down, she wasn't supposed to find Jaime again. Not yet.

Maybe, later on, Hazel would want to search for her mother. Or maybe their summer together would be all they'd ever have.

Either way, Hazel knew she'd be okay. She knew that things had a way of working out, even if it wasn't how, or when, she thought they might.

Hazel got dressed and went into the bathroom to brush her teeth. She pulled her hair out of the ponytail she'd stuck it in before bed. It hadn't grown an inch, and was still dyed platinum blond. She couldn't wait for it to grow out.

As she turned to leave the room, her eyes fell on the Polaroid in the corner. The picture of Wendy holding her on her hip. She'd never noticed how happy Wendy had looked. She'd wanted to be a mother, and she'd been able to make that dream come true, even if it was only for a little while.

She heard the familiar voices of Roy's favorite sportscasters on the TV downstairs. He'd been sleeping when she got in last night. She wasn't sure she'd be able to handle any kind of small talk when she'd walked in the door, and was relieved she hadn't had to.

But there was something almost like a smile on her face as she rounded the corner into the living room. There he was, as always, leaning against one corner of the couch, eyes fixed on the television and a bowl of cereal on his knee.

"Morning," he said, wiping the corner of his mouth and checking his beard for drops of stray milk. He scrambled for the remote and turned the volume down.

"Good morning," she said back. She couldn't believe it, but she kind of wanted to hug him. And if she'd been able to think of a single good excuse, or acceptable thing to say afterward, she probably would have done just that.

Instead, she smiled and made her way to the kitchen. The box of Cheerios was waiting for her on the table, next to a bowl and a spoon. She found the milk and fixed herself a bowl, hovering for a minute by the sink, before taking her breakfast back into the living room and settling onto the other side of the couch.

She could feel Roy watching her as she ate. He looked afraid to say anything, afraid to make her leave. Her eyes were frozen on the flashing screen, meaningless statistics scrolling across the bottom, over disconnected images of the weekend's Top Ten.

"Supposed to be nice out today," Roy said, glancing up at the window and squinting at the sun. "You think the rain will ever stop for good?"

Hazel followed his gaze out to the street and nodded. "I have a feeling we've seen the worst of it," she said, and took another soupy bite. She couldn't remember the last time she'd said so many words to him at once.

If he noticed, he did his best not to let on, just slurped the rest of his cereal and patted the arm of the sofa. "All righty then," he said, heaving himself up and dropping his bowl in the sink.

Hazel searched for the remote and flipped off the TV as Roy put on his hat and stood by the door.

"Guess you don't want a ride," he said, but it sounded like a question.

"No, thanks." She shrugged. "I'll just take the bus."

She tried to say it through a smile and hoped he knew it

wasn't about him. She had some things to sort out before she got to school. It had been one long weekend.

"All righty." Roy nodded, turning the knob and starting outside.

"Hey, Roy." Hazel stood up, knocking her leg against the coffee table.

Roy stopped and turned back over his shoulder. "Yeah?"

Hazel tugged the sleeves of her sweater over her thumbs. "I just wanted to say, you know," she stuttered, her heart skipping, her palms growing damp. There were all kinds of things she wanted to say, only they were piling up on top of each other and she wasn't sure she'd be able to separate them into coherent, speakable thoughts.

"I just wanted to tell you," she started again, taking a deep breath and sighing it out. "Keep the beard. I like it."

Roy tugged at his chin, smoothing the rusty hair along his jaw. "You think?"

Hazel nodded once, all business. "Definitely."

Roy flashed a quick smile, rapping his knuckles against the side of the door. "All righty," he said again, and pulled the door shut.

Hazel finished the last of her cereal and washed her bowl first, then Roy's, and put them both in the rack. She grabbed one of her old backpacks from the closet, found her books by the steps, and hurried outside for the bus.

She rushed to the end of her block, her shoulders falling as she watched the bus snake three blocks ahead, dusty red brake lights disappearing into traffic.

"Hey," she heard a voice call from behind her. "Wait up!"

Hazel stopped at the curb and turned to find Jasper Greene starting down the sidewalk. "Jasper?"

He slowed before he reached her, his crooked, heart-shaped smile twitching in place. "Trying to ditch me already?" he asked.

"Ditch you?" Hazel repeated. Like a flash, she remembered seeing him in the city. The books. The picture. She even remembered he'd said something to make her blush. What was it?

"It's Monday, isn't it?" Jasper asked. He was wearing dark jeans and an old cowboy shirt, with shiny buttons and inside-out stitching on the pocket. Hazel looked at him, his big brown eyes and funny hair, and realized she hadn't really seen him before.

"Isn't it?" he asked again, and this time it sounded like he could be wrong. She watched as his smile faded just slightly, the corners of his lips tightening, just the way Luke's had when she'd suddenly done or said something to make him nervous. "I thought we could ride together on the bus."

Hazel took a deep breath and tucked a piece of hair behind one ear. She looked up and down the street. She'd missed the first bus, and if they waited for the next one, they'd be late for homeroom.

"No," she said, shaking her head. Jasper looked at the sidewalk and kicked his leather shoe against the curb. He let out a long, heavy sigh, and Hazel realized what she'd said.

"No, I mean, no, we can't take the bus!" She laughed. "We missed it. We have to walk."

Jasper laughed, too, his smile back in place. "That's cool," he said. "I don't mind walking."

Hazel felt a familiar tug at her heart and realized that she didn't mind, either.

They stood at the crosswalk, looking up at the red flashing signal. When it turned green, Jasper looked at her sideways.

"Ready?" he asked.

"I'm ready," Hazel answered, and together they stepped down off the curb and into the street.

Epilogue

The boat to the city slipped away from Marin, shuttling commuters to work, students to their classes.

In the corner, by the door, a black canvas tote slumped against one wall. Spilling out of the bag was a dress: swirling, bright circles on slippery satin. Along the seam was a single, stubborn tear, and attached to the collar, a tag:

MARIPOSA OF THE MISSION

It was a dress that had been lost by those who no longer needed it, and it waited to be found by a girl who did. A girl in need of a second chance, or the courage to make her dreams come true. A girl with a wish in her heart.

Acknowledgments

Many thanks to many people:

To the ladies of Alloy, especially Sara Shandler and Joelle Hobeika, who have been, from the beginning, the most incredible editors, teachers, and friends. Also to Kristin Marang, who patiently introduced me to the Internet. It's an honor to have you all in my corner.

To the ladies of Scholastic, especially Aimee Friedman, Abby McAden, and Sheila Marie Everett, for your brilliant guidance and overwhelming support. (And for the coaching, talking-down-from-ledges, and reminders not to lose my conference badges. I'll try harder, I promise.)

To the remarkable David Levithan and his wonderful community of Young Adult writers, for welcoming me into the YA family. Most especially to Francisco X. Stork, for his beautiful books, and for showing me the ropes.

To the people of Martha's Vineyard: Setting this book on your island was a privilege. Special thanks to Madi and Bob Coutts, Erin Haggerty, Dana Inglehart, Nelia Decker and the West Tisbury library, Kristin Maloney and the Chilmark library, Cynthia Wolfson, and Zoe at Riley's Reads.

To my family of friends, Courtney Messinger and Alex Epton (for being my Brooklyn B&B), Hannah Kim, Katie Greisch, Jenna Bonistalli, Leah Tepper-Byrne, and Lauren O'Rourke. Thanks for keeping me around so long.

To Eliot, for reading a book about dresses in public, and for getting me out of the house.

As always, to my family: My mother, Maria Krokidas, for applying the "cry test" to countless drafts, and for reading my contracts so I don't have to. My father, Bruce Bullen, who gives the best advice. And to my brothers, George and John, for making me laugh, even when I don't feel like it.

This book is dedicated to my grandmothers, who lived across the street from each other the entire time I knew them, who always put their families first, and who are so much a part of what I write and the person I've turned out to be.

Thank you, thank you, thank you all.

More wishes. More dresses.
Don't miss

Wish

Another breathtaking novel by Alexandra Bullen

If you could have anything, what would you wish for?

Nothing can change the fact that Olivia Larsen's twin sister, Violet, is dead . . . until Olivia is given the change to make one wish—a wish that brings her sister back.

But Violet's return isn't what Olivia expected, and when she's granted two more wishes, things only get more complicated. As love, secrets, and a haunted past collide, Olivia realizes she must be careful what she wishes for . . . or her life will never be the same.

To Do List:
Read all the Point books!

Abandon
Airhead
Being Nikki
Runaway
By **Meg Cabot**

The Vampire Stalker
By **Allison Van Diepen**

Wish
Wishful Thinking
By **Alexandra Bullen**

Top 8
What's Your Status?
Unfriended
By **Katie Finn**

Sea Change
The Year My Sister Got Lucky
South Beach
French Kiss
Hollywood Hills
By **Aimee Friedman**

Clarity
Perception
By **Kim Harrington**

Ruined
Dark Souls
Unbroken
By **Paula Morris**

Possessed
Consumed
By **Kate Cann**

Suite Scarlett
Scarlett Fever
By **Maureen Johnson**

The Lonely Hearts Club
Prom and Prejudice
Take a Bow
By **Elizabeth Eulberg**

Wherever Nina Lies
By **Lynn Weingarten**